THE EARL IN MY BED

Also by Sophie Jordan

THE EARL IN MY BED

A Forgotten Princesses Valentine Novella

SOPHIE JORDAN

AVONIMPULSE
An Imprint of HarperCollins Publishers

Excerpt from *How to Lose a Bride in One Night* copyright © 2013 by Sharie Kohler.

Excerpt from *Firelight* copyright © 2010 by Sharie Kohler.

EPub Edition FEBRUARY 2013 ISBN: 9780062222466

Print Edition ISBN: 9780062222473

10 9 8 7 6 5 4 3 2

For my mother

CHAPTER ONE

She could delay no longer.

As much as she hoped to put it off another day, another fortnight, Paget could wait no longer. As it were, the winter winds might freeze her to the bones if she did not return home soon. With a heavy breath, she took the final step that brought her to the crest of the hill overlooking the sprawling manor house that belonged to the Earl of Winningham. Exposed to the elements atop the rise, her wool dress whipped around her legs.

Paget swallowed thickly. The earl himself was in residence. As he had been for the past month. He was all anyone discussed in the village. Every tongue wagged with his name. Speculation was ripe as to when he would surface. Whether he would attend Sunday service. Or even the annual Valentine's Day fête. Everyone desperately craved a glimpse of him.

Everyone except her.

She released a heavy breath, blowing aside a pale strand of hair that dangled in her face. Every Sunday she sat in the first pew, eyes trained on Papa at the head of the church, hands folded neatly in her lap as she braced herself for the telltale titter among the congregation, signaling the earl's long-anticipated arrival.

Thus far it had not occurred.

She fervently hoped he did not attend the baronet's Valentine fête. The annual gathering had always been such a happy time. Memories of it were always tangled up with her memories of Owen and Brand. Not Jamie. Never Jamie. *He* had never deigned to attend. He had looked down his aristocratic nose at such country gatherings. Only Owen and Brand had ever cared.

She blinked back the hot press of tears at the memory of her friends. Both were gone from her. One dead. The other fighting in a war halfway around the world. They should be here. Either one of them. *Both* of them.

An image of Jamie rose in her mind, that stiff walk of his with his hands clasped behind his back, his countenance dour, reflecting none of Brand's warmth or Owen's playfulness. He was the stiff, proper earl even when he had not been. Something dark twisted inside her heart. Perhaps he had always known the title would be his. Brand had always been weak and frail, after all.

Shaking off her bitter thoughts, she adjusted her grip on the basket handle. The aroma of warm biscuits drifted up to her nose as she sucked in a breath and descended the hill.

She wouldn't be the first to call upon him. Her father had done so, of course. An obligatory visit. She usually accompanied him on his calls, but on that occasion she'd stayed behind, blaming an aching head. Sitting in the Winningham's opulent drawing room without either Brand or Owen . . . knowing *Jamie* was the new earl . . .

She could not have borne it.

She still could not stomach it, but her father had looked askance at her when she declared that she would not be calling upon the earl with her customary basket of homemade lemon biscuits that she presented everyone with for all noteworthy occasions. The birth of a new child, the announcement of a betrothal, the passing of a relation. The new earl returning home after years of war certainly warranted a basket of baked goods, and well her father knew it. Well *she* knew it.

All was quiet in the morning light. Swans glided across the lake, faint ripples stretching out in ever-widening arcs. She eyed the manor's wide double doors as she approached.

The Earl of Winningham. *Jamie* was now the earl. This truth rattled around in her head as if looking for a place to settle. Dear, sweet Brand lay buried in the family cemetery on the other side of the sprawling manse. He'd never been long for this world. Never robust, never able to keep up and play with her or Owen. She and Owen always had to backtrack for him. For all that he had tried, Brand had always been more ghost than man.

Now the title belonged to Jamie. Taciturn and aggravatingly proper James. Always looking down at Owen. Always making certain Owen never forgot he was a mere half-brother. Always looking down at *her*, a mere vicar's daughter.

Unbidden, the memory flashed of Jamie happening upon Brand and Owen saddling mounts in the Winningham stable for an afternoon ride. She had stood alongside them, dancing in place, beyond excited. They promised to let her ride their new thoroughbred.

"Really, Brand. You're father's heir. You should know better than to consort with a girl of her ilk. I would expect such lack of judgment from Owen but not you."

She did not give Owen the chance to defend her before she sent a dried clod of manure smacking Jamie in the middle of the face. A wholly reckless thing to do. Even if she was only a child of tender years. She was the vicar's daughter. She should have known better. She should have regretted her actions and apologized immediately. But of course she had not.

Instead she'd planted her hands on her hips and thrust out her chin. "There's more where that came from, you stodgy prig!"

Jamie had brushed the filth from his face and looked down his arrogant nose at her. Only three years her senior, he towered over her. "And I believe that only proves my point at how very ill-suited you are to keep company with my brothers."

The rejoinder had hit its mark. It stung even now. She should have behaved better and shown just how dignified and gracious she could be . . . that it wasn't a trait reserved to the aristocracy as he seemed to think.

Now that haughty peacock was home while Brand was dead and Owen was left fighting in a rebellion across the ocean. It was vastly unfair.

She flexed her hands around the handle of her basket and knocked on the heavy front door.

Mr. Jarvis, the ancient butler, promptly answered.

"Miss Ellsworth," he greeted very properly, eyeing the length of her. His eyes brightened when they landed on the basket and she had no doubt he would filch one of her infamous biscuits from within before it ever made it to the earl's hands.

"Hello, Mr. Jarvis. Is Lord Winningham receiving?"

"He's not in at present." He paused, his gaze still fixed on her basket. "Shall I take your parcel? I'll see he gets it upon his return."

Her heart skipped with delight as she quickly passed the basket into the butler's hands. "Would you be so kind, Mr. Jarvis?"

She was cowardly, she knew, but she would not have to face him after all and feign happiness at his return. Relief coursed through her. She could rest easy and face her father having done her duty.

Jarvis nodded. "Quite so. Thank you, Miss Ellsworth. I'll see the basket is returned."

With a hasty wave and murmured thanks, she descended the wide front steps, her gaze skittering left and right as though the earl himself might appear and put a stop to her retreat.

With every step that distanced her from the estate, her breathing eased as the tension ebbed from her shoulders. At the crest of the hill, she paused beside the old oak and looked back, her hand curling into the rough bark as she stared at the sprawling manse that reeked of wealth and privilege.

Tears sprang to her eyes at the thought of Owen. He deserved to return home just as much as James did.

Please, let him be well. Safe. Alive and whole.

Again, she was struck with the unfairness of it all. Jamie had returned, but Owen remained in India, fighting for his life while servants waited hand and foot on his wretched brother. She read the papers. She knew of the atrocities being played out abroad. Civilians were not spared. She could not fathom how dangerous it was for a soldier.

Swiping at her eyes, she edged back a step, eager to be gone from the house that filled her with such somber thoughts. Whenever she grew morose, she penned Owen a missive. Whether her letters actually reached him was doubtful, she knew. Or at least she surmised as much, given he had ceased to correspond back to her. She had received only three letters, in the beginning, years ago. Since then, nothing. And yet she still wrote him, telling herself that if he received even a fraction of them, she could be offering him much-needed comfort.

Sniffing back threatening tears, she nodded decisively. Fully intending to return home and write him a new letter, she spun around and smacked into a wall. Hard.

She staggered. Strong hands steadied her, singeing her through the sleeves of her cloak and dress.

A gasp escaped her. "Oh! Forgive—pardon—I wasn't—"

Her awkward apology died as her gaze lifted to the face in front of her. "Jamie," she said before she could consider that she should address him with more formality. Heat flooded her face. He was an earl now, and they had scarcely been friends before. On the contrary. He would expect her to be more circumspect.

"Miss Ellsworth." The proper, crisp pronouncement of her surname jarred her. His hands fell from her arms and he distanced himself with a smart step back. His voice was deeper than she remembered. She actually felt it. Like a physical touch . . . a feather stroke along her stretched nerves.

She blinked up at him, her head tilting back. Was he always this tall?

She had braced herself for this moment. Even as unwanted as it was, she knew it would come. She would see him somewhere about the village. Still ... she was not prepared for this sight of him.

Gone was the gangly young lordling she remembered. The pup, it seemed, had grown into his limbs and paws.

"Lord Winningham." This time she managed a more proper tone.

They stood awkwardly, staring at one another. His face was harder, carved granite. His skin sun-kissed. Then it occurred to her that he didn't appear awkward at all. That condition seemed reserved for her alone. He seemed perfectly at ease and comfortable within his skin. He looked her up and down mildly. She detected faint curiosity brimming in his blue-green eyes as he assessed the changes that four years had wrought.

She tried not to fidget, smoothing her hands against her sides. She doubted she had changed much. She was merely an older version of the girl he and Owen had left behind. He, without a thought. Owen, with a kiss. Her first and last since.

She felt compelled to fill the silence. "You look ... well, my lord."

He looked more than *well*. She was loath to admit it—and a little startled at his impact on her—but he looked handsome. Strong and virile. Certain she did not look half so polished, she felt the insane need to reach up and tidy her hair.

He nodded brusquely but did not return the compliment. Of course not. That would require him to be polite to a person he deemed lesser then himself.

"My condolences on the passing of your brother, my

lord." She spoke the words because she must. Even though the condolences might be owed more to her. It was she who had kept Brand company these last years. While other girls in the village cavorted and made marriages for themselves, she had remained steadfast at Brand's side, reading to him and playing the pianoforte for him, watching him as he labored for breath. He had been so pale and frail at the end that she could not imagine what kept the air pumping out of his thin chest.

Her words failed to move him. The earl stared down at her, his expression bemused. As if he did not know her at all. And she supposed he did not. She had only spent every free moment with Owen and Brand since she was seven years old. *He*, in fact, did not know her. Not then. Not now.

He looked away from her then, his sea-colored eyes gazing off toward the house. She studied his profile, the sharp blade of his nose, the press of his well-carved lips. Even tightly set she could see the bottom lip was full. Another thing she had not noticed before. Surely his lips had not changed, too.

"For the best, I suppose," he murmured.

For the best? Brand's dying was for the best? He could not mean to say *that*.

With a hissing breath, she squared her shoulders. "Whatever do you mean?"

He faced her again, leveling those seawater eyes on her. "He had suffered quite long enough—"

"I can assure you that he did not think dying was for the best."

He angled his head, his expression growing rather intense as he studied her. That much hadn't changed. He had always looked at her with such intense eyes. Always so serious. Even as children. "Indeed?"

She continued, "As you were not here, allow me to enlighten you." Unfair, she supposed, to fling that accusation at him. He couldn't really be blamed for being away at war, could he? If she blamed him for that, she must blame Owen, too.

He settled back on his heels. The action seemed to make him look only more formidable. His chest vast, broader. "Pray continue."

"Brand did not want to die. His spent every breath fighting for the next. He wanted to live." Hot emotion burned though her, scalding her all the way to her eyes, but she could not stop. "He talked of tomorrow. Of what he wanted to do. Marriage. Children. Of seeing Owen again." Her lip curled ever so faintly. "Of even seeing you, my lord."

Something passed over his countenance. Anger? Hurt? Regret? It was gone too quickly for her to identify. And then she dismissed it entirely. Staring at his implacable expression, the flatness of his gaze, she knew her words had not affected him.

He inhaled. "I suppose I owe you for those long hours at my brother's bedside, Miss Ellsworth."

She pulled back in affront. "*Owe* me?"

"Yes. I dare not assume your time and attention to Brand was without value. You were here for him when no other relations happened to be. I'm more than happy to compensate you—"

Her hand lashed out. She could not stop herself. Could not even think before her palm connected with his cheek with a sharp *crack*.

His head whipped to the side. Instantly, a white hand-print marked his swarthy cheek.

Horror washed over her. Her palm stung where she'd connected with his face.

His eyes glittered as he looked down at her, his fingers lightly fingering his afflicted cheek. "Some things, it seems, have not changed overly much."

Chapter Two

She did not confuse his meaning. Or his smug tone. He meant *she* had not changed. In his eyes, she was the little heathen he'd always judged her to be.

Still fuming over his offer to compensate her for attending to Brand, her *friend*, she ignored the voice inside her that insisted she apologize.

"On the contrary." She nodded, her fury still smoldering. "Things change all the time. *People* change." She very deliberately raked him with her gaze. "They become worse."

More arrogant. More unbearable.

He dropped his hand from his face, his seawater eyes frigid as they roamed over her.

With a hot exhale, she nodded stiffly. "Good day, my lord."

She strode past him, her strides cutting angrily as she began to descend the hill. That had gone even worse than she imagined possible. She had actually struck him. She would need to apologize. Only not now. Now she couldn't. She simply had to get away.

His deep voice called after her, "Do you not even care enough to inquire after Owen?"

It was the one question that could stop her in her tracks. She halted, her spine rigid. She didn't want to rise to the bait. She didn't want to turn and face him again. She winced.

Nor did she not want to miss out on anything he could impart about Owen. Whether, for instance, he had received any of her countless letters.

She turned slowly and walked back toward him. Her gaze scanned his face. Something twisted inside her at the red handprint on his cheek.

She moistened her lips. "How is he?"

"Alive," he rejoined, his voice flat. "At least the last time I saw him." So cold. So matter of fact. Did he not even care?

"Does he . . ." *Speak of me?* She wanted to say it, wanted to ask, but could not bear to utter the words and all it would reveal of her. All the doubt and uncertainty she felt toward the boy she had loved all her life. The boy she had imagined she would marry someday. For no one had ever understood and accepted her the way Owen had . . . a girl more comfortable running barefoot on the hills. It seemed only natural that they should always be together. Natural to her and everyone else.

Instead, she asked, "Does he receive my letters?"

Jamie stared at her, his gaze penetrating. "Yes."

Hurt flashed through her. *And he never wrote.* No matter the doubts she harbored for their future—if they should actually *marry* each other—she still cared for him. He could have penned at least one letter. "All of them?"

"Well, I cannot know how many you wrote, can I?" he countered.

She felt herself flush. "No. Of course not." He continued to stare at her, waiting, but she did not care to elaborate and admit she wrote him every week. Sometimes more. At least in the beginning.

Of late she had not mailed half the missives she penned . . . hating to think they went unread. She wrote them and locked them in her desk.

And there was something she could barely admit to herself. She was afraid that if she did mail them, they might reach Owen. He would read her words and sense that she wasn't the same girl he'd left behind. Perhaps, in the scrawl of her script, in the words spoken and unspoken, he would hear that she wasn't certain they were quite so perfect for each other anymore. That what they once had was nothing more than the fancy of childhood. Perhaps he would detect her hope that he had forgotten his commitment and devotion to her.

"He wrote in the beginning." She moistened her lips. "Has something happened to make him stop?"

"Yes." He paused, frowning at her, looking at her as though she was dim-witted. "War happened."

She nodded, staring down at her hands, feeling wretched. "Of course. I should have realized."

As if he possessed insight into her thoughts, the earl stepped closer, murmuring softly, "He has not forgotten you."

She drew a quick, hissing breath. The words fell heavily upon her, a burden she did not wish to bear. Doubtlessly, the earl thought he was offering her solace. On the contrary. It felt as though a noose had just tightened about her neck.

"That is . . . ." She groped for the right word. "That is good to hear."

"I'm sure your eventual reunion will be most happy." With a wince, he lifted a hand to his cheek. "No doubt different from our own."

Familiar heat crept up her neck to her cheeks. Suddenly an apology was not too difficult to perform. "That was not well done of me."

He inclined his head. "I offended."

He was apologizing? She angled her head to the side, studying him, quite certain the Jamie of old had never apologized for anything. Especially not to the likes of her.

They remained where they were, a respectable distance between them in the vast space of the outdoors, yet an air of intimacy cloaked the exchange. Her fingers tapped nervously at her side. The wind lifted loose tendrils of hair and whipped them across her face, reminded her how unkempt she must appear. She gathered them with one hand and tucked the pale strands behind her ear.

Her pulse stuttered anxiously in her neck. "I hope you're acclimating well to home, Lord Winningham."

"As well as can be expected when I'm to fill the shoes of a much grieved brother. All while I've left the other one to risk his neck on a battlefield a world away. I feel a villain in a very bad drama."

She blinked. "You do not mince speech."

He lifted one shoulder. "To what point? I can see in your eyes what so many others already think."

She squared her shoulders. "And what is that?"

He stepped closer. She held her ground.

His gaze flicked over her, just a quick, cursory examination before settling back on her face. He peered into her eyes as if confirming for himself that the nameless sentiment to which he referred was there. "You think it should be me rotting in the earth. Or on the battlefield. Whatever the case, I don't belong or deserve to be here."

She sucked in a breath.

He smiled mirthlessly, those well-carved lips curving upward. "Come. Don't look so shocked." He pressed a finger beneath her chin and closed her mouth for her.

Heat and awareness spread from that single point of contact. She jerked back a step. "I'm certain that's not t-true."

"I've never been anyone's favorite." He looked into her eyes meaningfully, and she knew he was implying that he had never been *her* favorite. And how could she deny the allegation? It was true.

"Do you want to be?" she challenged, knowing the answer already. He did not.

He had never behaved as one hoping to win the favor of others.

The sudden gleam in his eyes told her he knew this, too.

"My father will be missing me. It was lovely to see you again, Lord Winningham." Oh, how the title still stuck in her throat. Turning, she moved away, not waiting for his response.

She thought she heard his murmured farewell, and something else, other words lost on the wind. Her nape tingled and she brushed her hand there, certain that it was his gaze she felt.

She quickened her pace.

Jamie watched the vicar's daughter hasten away. His lips twisted wryly. He suspected she would run if she could. If it wouldn't be a complete break in decorum, she'd lift her skirts and race from him as quickly as her feet would carry her.

She was everything and more than he remembered. The defiance was still there. That stubborn angle to her chin. The sparkling light in her brown-black eyes. She was a tightly wound package, her feisty nature threatening to spill free. He studied her trim shape marching briskly away. She was still the girl who had thrown manure in his face.

He winced at the memory. He'd deserved it. He'd been such an arrogant pup, full of jealousy. It was a bitter thing to feel like an outsider among your own family. But it had always been that way. His place had always been rather hazy in his mind. Brand was the heir, and Owen the beloved son from his father's second marriage . . . a love union. Owen even possessed a title. He was Lord McDowell, having inherited a Scottish earldom through his mother.

Jamie had always felt unnecessary. Easily overlooked. The fact that Brand and Owen preferred each other—and even the vicar's daughter—only drove home his sense of isolation among his own family.

And then there was Paget Ellsworth. Hoyden and all-around trouble. His brothers adored her. Followed her about like puppies. Not him. Even if they had made room for him in their cozy little trio, he had refused to be another to dote upon her.

Blasted pride. He'd felt a resurgence of it today, prompting him to provoke her. He shook his head, and clasped his hands behind his back. He'd come far. Years had passed. He would not allow himself to feel the old disgruntlement. Brand was gone. And Owen . . .

A sour taste coated his mouth. He was still over there. Fighting for his life. Jamie had been forced home. He'd tried to stay, unwilling to leave Owen, but the colonel had demanded it of him once they received word of Brand's death. He closed his eyes in a long blink and shook his head, fighting off the memory of their final encounter. The dead look in Owen's eyes as he turned from Jamie.

"*You'll be home soon, Owen*," he had called, the promise feeble even to his ears.

Owen did not look back, merely moved forward with hard strides, his rifle slung over his shoulder. He fell into step with four other soldiers from the regiment who had been singled out for their excellent marksmanship. They were leaving to hunt down rebel sepoys who had taken prisoner several merchants and their families. It was a kill mission. His brother had become quite skilled at those. He was used almost exclusively as an assassin.

He doubted Miss Ellsworth would even know Owen when he returned. He was not the same boy who had left her.

Jamie opened his eyes again and gazed after Miss Ellsworth's retreating figure. At least she had not changed. He took satisfaction in that. She had grown into just the kind of woman he had imagined. Passionate. Strong. Full of life.

The kind of woman Owen deserved to come home to. The kind who could remind him of life and happiness and make him forget the dark days that demanded he kill or be killed.

The kind of female Jamie intended to keep at arm's length. No matter how much she fascinated him.

No matter how much she always had.

Dear Owen,

*I saw Jamie today. The sight of him hale and hearty
fills me with confidence that you are well and will soon be
returned to us. He says you receive my letters so I pray they
bring you some comfort. I know you'll be home soon and we
may once again . . .*

Paget paused over the page, unsure what to write, what to
say next. She did not wish to make any promises, nor could
she be anything less than warm and affectionate. Not while
he struggled for survival a continent away. She wouldn't be
that cruel. Or callous. She needed to give him hope and en-
couragement.

Sighing, she rose from the desk, determining to finish the
missive later. A walk would clear her thoughts. While the
weather held at any rate. A low, gray sky had hung about all
morning, threatening to trap her indoors the remainder of
the day. She'd let gray skies bully her no longer.

She passed the housekeeper, Mrs. Donnelly, in the narrow
hall. "I'm going for a stroll."

"It's going to rain," Mrs. Donnelly cautioned.

"I'll be quick."

Mrs. Donnelly shook her steel-gray head. "You'll get
yourself soaked."

At the door, Paget flung her cloak around her shoulders
and pulled up the hood. "It won't be the first time. If I wait for
a sunny day, I should never step outside."

Mrs. Donnelly awarded Paget with one of her less-than-
fierce scowls. After all these years, the glares failed to instill
fear in Paget. With so few memories of her own mother,

Mrs. Donnelly had served in that capacity ... and never having children of her own, she was a tad indulgent.

"You'll not look so cheeky when you're brought low with the ague. Aye, you'll likely be dead."

"True." Paget nodded grimly. "I rather suppose I won't look cheeky from within my grave."

"Ah, you impudent lass. Hurry on with you, then. Perhaps you will beat the coming deluge." She stabbed the air in the direction of a window.

"I won't go far," she promised with a smile as she stepped out into the murky morning. She took off at a fast clip, her mind drifting back to the half-written letter she'd left on her desk.

Her thoughts didn't linger there long, however, before sliding in another direction. James. *Jamie.* No—the Earl of Winningham. She must remember him as such. It wouldn't do to slip and address him so informally again.

She pulled her fur-lined hood over her head. Her body soon warmed as her legs trod over the familiar road. She came to the part of the road lined with apple trees. In the winter, their barren branches met and tangled together overhead to create a canopied effect. Even skeletal, she still loved the stretch of trees. It was one of her first memories upon arriving in Winninghamshire.

She recalled driving down the lane with her parents on either side of her and looking up at the canopy of branches. It had been wondrous. More dream than real. She had felt as if she stumbled into one of the fairy tales her mother told her before bed. The apple trees had been in full bloom. A gentle breeze sent petals fluttering through the air. Several had caught in her lashes and she fancied she was entering the realm of some fairy kingdom. When she first spotted the Winningham manor, she was certain of it. She'd imagined a princess lived in the great stone mausoleum and had been quite disappointed to learn only princes resided within. Three princes much too old for her to play with. She smiled ruefully. In the beginning at any rate. At age six, Owen had no time for a three-year-old. However, by the time she was seven, there was nowhere she went without Owen and Brand. The ever-taciturn Jamie had kept to himself.

Carriage wheels sounded behind her, coupled with the steady clump of hooves. She stepped to the side of the road and paused, recognizing Sir John's conveyance. It slowed to a stop as it came abreast of her.

The baroness stuck her head out the window, a ridiculous confection perched precariously atop her head. This one was more feathers than hat.

"Paget! What are you doing? It looks to rain! Come within at once."

Paget smiled at her friend. "I'm fine. I'll be home before the rain arrives."

Alice Mary rolled her eyes. "You always say that and then end up soaked."

Paget frowned. Had Alice Mary and Mrs. Donnelly been talking?

Sir John then peered out the carriage window beside his wife, the two of them crowding the frame. "Indeed, join us, Miss Ellsworth. We can see you home."

"Better yet, return home with us," Alice Mary encouraged with an eager bobbing of her head. "I've countless tasks to prepare yet for the ball and could use your assistance. Now that the wretched Earl of Winningham accepted our invitation, I can delay no longer."

"Come now, dearest," her husband chided.

Alice Mary pouted. "I know it's uncharitable, but he has never been a particular favorite of mine. He was always so mean to Paget . . . looking down his nose at her. At all of us in the village. Remember, Paget? I dread seeing him again."

Paget nodded, not bothering to reveal she had already seen the earl. That would only sentence her to an inquisition.

"He's just reserved in nature, dear," Sir John offered.

"You are too kind, husband. Aloof and rude is a more accurate description." She sighed. "But no fear. I shall be a consummate hostess and don a smile even for the likes of him. Oh, so many decisions yet . . . Shall the ice sculpture be a Cupid? Or is that too passé?" She wrinkled her pert little nose. "I was thinking the gentlemen might find a sculpture of Aphrodite much more diverting. I don't want this to be like any Valentine's ball before—" Alice Mary brushed a conciliatory hand against her husband's cheek. "No offense intended, darling."

A smile twitched Paget's lips, perfectly aware that Alice Mary's apology was in reference to the fact that Sir John's mother had planned the ball in previous years. This was Alice Mary's first year as the new baroness. Paget knew taking the reins from her mother-in-law filled Alice Mary with equal parts delight and trepidation.

Sir John took his wife's hand and pressed a fervent kiss to the back of her glove. His eyes glowed with his usual devotion and something else. Something secret and deep.

Paget fidgeted, her face warming.

"Of course not, darling," Sir John assured.

Alice Mary blushed prettily, basking in her husband's adoration.

Paget cleared her throat, feeling awkward—not a new sensation when she was around her childhood friend lately. When she was in the company of her new husband, Alice Mary was no longer the same girl. Since she'd become the baronet's wife—a definite coup for the daughter of the village's only physician—an invisible barrier had risen between them. All at once she was a matron whilst Paget was still a maid. And not just any matron, but a glowing matron with secret smiles.

Paget knew it was only partly because Alice Mary was now a married lady while she was not. It was more because Alice Mary was a *happily* married lady. A happily besotted, cannot-stand-to-be-apart-from-her-husband lady.

Quite simply, they were enamored of one another. Paget suspected this was the grand passion she read about in novels. It was there, evident in their shared glances, the small touches between them. The very air around them was charged with something even Paget, for all her ignorance on the matter, recognized as desire.

It intrigued her. Her single kiss with Owen had been nice . . . but, well . . .

She yearned for more than *nice*.

She wanted what Alice Mary had and that wasn't something she could ever have with Owen. He was like a brother to her. Not a lover. In his absence, she had come to realize this. She only hoped he had reached the same realization in the years since he left Winninghamshire. She did not wish to hurt him.

Alice Mary tore her gaze away from her husband, appearing to suddenly remember Paget's presence. She motioned for her to join them. "Come now, Join me—"

"Thank you, but I told Mrs. Donnelly I'd be home shortly. I wouldn't want to alarm her."

"Oh, very well. But you must call on me this week. The sooner the better. I really need you, Paget. Decisions must be made. I haven't a moment more to spare."

Paget smiled, doubting very much her friend *needed* her to make such weighty decisions as what type of ice sculpture she should commission, but she would humor her. "Of course. I promise."

"Very well. Enjoy your walk." She glanced to the skies. "Were I you, I would hasten for home."

Paget nodded, but overtly avoided agreeing. "I shall call on you tomorrow."

Satisfied, Alice Mary nodded and sat back in her seat. Sir John called out farewell and knocked on the ceiling. The carriage lurched forward.

Paget watched as the newlyweds rounded the lane and vanished from sight. Instead of turning for home, she set out across the countryside, burrowing deeper into her cloak and relishing the bite of wind on her cheeks that made her feel so very alive. She ignored the darkening skies, telling herself she would turn back for home soon. She simply wished to walk off some of her restlessness. An unidentifiable energy buzzed through her. Her strides quickened as if she could somehow exorcise the sensation from her limbs and imbue herself with the serenity that had once ruled her.

For some reason an image of the earl rose in her mind. She snorted. Of all men, he shouldn't be the one to occupy her thoughts. So he was handsome . . . and virile. He wasn't the only gentleman in these parts, and he certainly was not the one to cure her restless nature. It was purely coincidence that her encounter with him coincided with her longing for . . . something. For more. Adventure. Excitement. An end to her dull existence.

Her breath fell harder as she walked. As if she could forget her encounter with the earl and Alice Mary and Sir John and the longing consuming her. As if she could once again be satisfied with her life.

CHAPTER THREE

The rain fell in heavy sheets, coloring the landscape an opaque gray. Jamie squinted against the deluge and wiped at his face. It did little good. Visibility was still low.

He'd departed early this morning on foot to visit Mrs. Neddles, his former nurse. Now almost eighty, she lived a village over from Winninghamshire. She was still as sharp as ever. He'd never forgotten her. She'd done a great deal for him, especially after his father remarried and Owen came along—when Jamie often felt invisible, lost in the middle of Brand and the new son. Mrs. Neddles had given him additional affection and always tried to lure him from his shell.

In the gray haze, he spotted a tight copse of trees in the near distance. He vaguely recalled it from his youth. It would do until the worst of the storm broke.

The rain pelted him like icy needles as he strode ahead, mindful of where he stepped on the spongy ground.

At the fringe of the copse, the ends of the branches gathered close and dipped low. He ducked his head as he stepped beneath the canopy.

Immediately he was protected from the worst of the rain. Water dripped sporadically through the ceiling of tightly tangled leaves and branches. The world seemed quieter, the patter of rain a distant thing under the umbrella of foliage.

He assessed his surroundings. The copse consisted of four or five trees hugged close together. A giant oak, too large for him to even wrap his arms around, loomed like a parent over the others.

He approached, contemplating settling his back against it, when a figure stepped out from the other side of it.

Deep brown eyes blinked at him in surprise. A surprise that only mirrored his own.

Paget peered up at him. "My lord . . ."

"Miss Ellsworth. What are you doing here?"

She lifted a slim gloved hand, her voice lifting above the patter of rain. "I imagine doing the same thing you are . . . s-seeking shelter until the rain dissipates." Her teeth chattered, a testament that not only was she wet but cold.

The hem of her cloak—and what he could detect of her dress—was muddied almost to the knees. With her hood pushed back, the ties pulled at her throat, reddening her flesh. He imagined the hood was heavy from rainwater.

"I would offer you my coat, but I feel it is as wet as your cloak."

She shook her head. "Quite right, but I thank you for the thought."

"You are welcome."

An awkward silence sank between them as the words of their polite exchange faded.

Wild strands of hair spilled loose to frame her face. Wet

as it was, the pale hair appeared almost brown. She was a mess and seemed to know it. Her hand patted at her hair as if that would help tidy the damage. Her dark eyes darted from him to the ground and back again. As if she did not know quite where to look.

It wasn't the first time he'd witnessed her in a state of disarray. This was the Paget who climbed trees with Owen. But she'd been a girl then.

She was no longer that barely-out-of-the-schoolroom girl he'd last seen. She was a woman now and a feast for his eyes. His gaze strayed to the gentle swell of breasts pressing against the wet bodice of her dress. Gooseflesh puckered the milk skin there. His body immediately responded. His cock stirred against his trousers. With a mental curse, he jerked his gaze out at the horizon. The branches hung low, obscuring anything above shoulder-view and granting him only a limited glimpse of the landscape.

He inhaled deeply. They were well-shrouded from the world. Not that there was likely to be any other passersby even if they were not. Not in this storm. A fact that filled him with apprehension. He was alone, isolated with the first female to rouse his interest since returning to England.

Her soft voice stroked his frayed nerves. "I was warned that it would rain—"

"And still you decided for a stroll?" he countered, his voice sharper than he intended.

He had not anticipated another encounter with her so soon. After the last, she'd found her way into his thoughts far too often. If he wasn't careful he might form an attachment. Unacceptable, that. She belonged to Owen. She always had. And when he returned home there would be nothing to keep them apart. No war. Not the span of a continent. And certainly not him.

The color rose in her cheeks. "As did you," she replied hotly.

"I set out at dawn with no notion that the weather would take such a turn. You'd do well to take care of yourself lest you hope to sicken." He snorted. "Wouldn't that be some tragic irony? Owen returning home to an ailing . . ." His voice faded as something flashed in the dark of her eyes.

She angled her head to the side. "An ailing . . . *what?*"

Precisely. What term could he apply to her? He shook his head and looked out again at the water-washed land.

He *felt* her step closer. "Pray continue. What were you going to say?"

"Do I need to say it?"

"I wish you would."

He whipped his head back to stare down at her. The sight of her gleaming dark eyes—always a bit otherworldly even when they were children, like a beast of the forest thrust amid mortal man—only managed to infuriate him more. It was her eyes he remembered most. The vast depth of her stare, the penetrating dark that swallowed him whole even now, made him feel exposed. As though there was no hiding from her. A terrifying prospect. And yet also tempting. That she might recognize his loneliness.

And his sudden desire for her.

It should shame him and make him turn from her but he held his ground, scanning her slight frame from head to toe, his imagination running, envisioning her stripped free of her sodden clothing. His palms tingled at the notion of removing the pins from her wet hair and letting the pale length fall around her body like Botticelli's Venus. He was being foolish, of course. A woman of her inexperience wouldn't recognize his interest in her. And coming from him, Paget surely would not expect it. Not with their past. "Owen and I fought side by side for years. We came to rely on each other out there."

She nodded.

He continued, "We may have not been the closest children, but there's little I don't know when it comes to him now."

She blinked. "I never implied you and he—"

"Suffice to say I'm aware of the regard you hold for each other. When he comes home, he'll be coming home for you."

She inhaled and stepped back. A flicker of something he thought to be unease passed over her expression. "But there is no understanding between Owen and myself."

He let loose a single rough bark of laughter. Was she really that naïve? "Indeed? For God's sake. Paget, there doesn't need to be a declaration. Sometimes words aren't necessary. You will marry, of course. Everyone knows this. Don't tell me you do not?"

Color stained her cheeks and she glanced away as if unable to meet his gaze—or answer his question. He watched her swallow, the damp skin of her throat working.

His palms tingled and he curled his fingers into a fist, stopping himself from pushing back the wet tendrils that clung to that tempting expanse of skin.

Immediately, the thought of his mouth there, tasting her neck for himself, followed. He squeezed his eyes in a hard, punishing blink.

Such thoughts were . . . unthinkable. He was only tormenting himself. She'd likely slap him a second time. As she should. He'd do well to find a willing female and slake his lusts . . . forgetting about this inconvenient attraction.

"I—" she started to say in a small voice before pausing. She began again, her voice stronger, "It's not like that between Owen and me."

He could only stare at her for a moment, her words sinking in slowly. "What are you saying?" A dangerous sense of foreboding crept over him, sliding up his nape and tightening his scalp.

"I cannot consider him as . . . as a woman *should* consider a man she's to one day marry."

He took a swift step forward and she took a hasty step back.

She must have seen something in his expression . . . some of the anger coming over him. She stared up at him with wide eyes.

He stopped, holding up a hand as though to pacify her. "You cannot mean that." He shook his head slowly. "You'll destroy him."

"I've tried to will myself to feel differently!" She shook her head. "I cannot feel what is not there." She looked up at him with large, pleading eyes.

He turned away. "I don't care to hear this," he muttered. The image of his brother as he'd last seen him, haggard and dead-eyed, exhausted from their last campaign where half their company had been decimated flashed through his mind. The guilt he'd felt on leaving had only been mollified by his conviction that Owen would soon be home. And Paget Ellsworth would be waiting for him.

She came after him, her icy-cold hand falling on his wrist, pulling him back around to face her. "Who else should I talk to? You're his brother. You've seen him recently . . . you can tell me how I should best approach—"

"No," he bit out. "Don't ask me the best way to destroy my brother."

Her hand dropped from his arm. "I cannot love him . . . not as he deserves."

"Try harder," he growled.

"I've thought long over the kiss we shared when he left . . . it was not . . . it's not . . ." She lightly brushed her fingers over her lips, as though she still tasted their farewell kiss there.

His stomach knotted as he gazed at those lips. The thin upper lip and plumper bottom. It was an elegant mouth. Demure and dusky pink. But he could well imagine it a deeper shade, red and swollen from kissing.

He jerked away and dragged his hands though his hair, ridding his mind of that image before facing her again. "You're letting silly, girlhood notions fill your head."

She squared her shoulders, her tone sharp with indignation. "I know my heart. I love Owen, but only as a friend . . . as a brother."

He shook his head, thinking of Owen spinning fantasies of her as he fought for his life. She would never find a more worthy man. "You're an idiot," he snapped.

Her mouth sagged at the insult. With a blink, she regained her composure. "I don't have to stand here and listen to this." She marched past him.

He closed his eyes in a pained blink. Perhaps he could have spoken with more tact. "Where are you going?"

"Home," she called over her shoulder.

"It's still pouring." He strode after her, motioning to the rain-drenched landscape.

"I don't care. Better a soaking than remain here for your abuse."

He seized her arm. She whirled around and struck him in the chest with her fist. "Unhand me, you brute!"

He caught her offending fist, small and cold in his grip. She pulled back her other arm and he caught that wrist, too. She glared up at him. Her chest heaved, lifting her breasts high against her bodice. It wasn't a deliberate move. It couldn't be. She didn't know what she was doing . . . she could not fathom her effect on him. That every inch of him was wound tight and aching, suffering from her nearness. God, he needed release. A soft, willing body to ease him and banish her from his thoughts.

He fought for restraint, for calm, and swallowed deeply. "You're romanticizing marriage—"

"I am not. I want passion. Desire."

He snorted. "You've been reading too many novels, Miss Ellsworth."

"Please remove that smirk from your face. It exists. I know it does."

"Do you now?" An ugly suspicion took root. "Have you already found someone then to share this grand passion with you?"

He couldn't say why, but he held his breath, feeling dangerously out of sorts as he awaited her answer . . . certain that if she said yes he would find the bastard and thrash him to an inch of his life.

"No."

Relief coursed through him.

"But it exists," she insisted. "I know it. I've seen proof in others. And if I'm not to have it with my husband, then where else shall I find it?"

A strained silence fell between them. Where indeed? She stared up at him, waiting for him to answer. Her gaze scanned his face, lingering on his mouth with a rapt fascination that tightened his skin. Was she even aware of where she was looking—and how it affected him?

"What of friendship? Loyalty?" His voice wrenched from deep in his throat, low and strained as he watched her watching him ... his mouth. "Are those not sentiments valued within marriage?"

Her eyes flicked back to his. She looked troubled for a moment, and hope flared within him that he was getting through to her. He pushed his advantage. "You can't crush Owen like this ..."

She wet her lips. He followed the movement of her tongue, and something twisted inside of him.

"What of me? What of my needs?" She wiggled her wrist in his grip, but still he clung. "Shall I pretend each time we're together that he makes my heart race when I feel nothing more than friendship? Is that honest?" she continued, her voice a soft rasp. "Is that fair to him? It has been four years, Jamie."

"I don't find most women overly concerned with honesty when it comes to dealings with the opposite sex. Why should it concern you?"

"Oh! You're insufferable."

"Friendship is more than many people ever find in a spouse."

Her mouth thinned into a stubborn line. "Well, I want more than that."

His anger mounting, he asked, "Aren't you so very fortunate that you can afford to be so selfish?"

An outraged huff of breath escaped her. "You don't understand. You would have to possess a heart . . . and *feelings*. All of which you clearly lack." She pulled free and spun around again. She was almost clear of the overhanging branches when he caught her again.

It occurred to him he should just allow her to go. Until he thought of Owen, and the rejection he would face upon his return. He needed her to see reason . . .

He wrapped a hand around her waist and pulled her back beneath the canopy of leaves. She struggled against him as he carried her deeper within the copse and dropped her so that she was pressed against the tree.

Her dark eyes glittered with outrage. "How dare you?"

"Passion . . . desire . . . it's not all it's made out to be. It fades. Usually after the first taste."

"Not when it's combined with love," she countered.

He rolled his eyes. "Oh, you want love, too? You might as well wish for the moon. You'll toss aside Owen on a fantasy."

"I can't change the way I feel," she said through clenched teeth. "*You* can't change the way I feel."

Can't he?

Frustration rose up inside him as he stared down at her upturned face.

"No?" he growled. "Perhaps I can prove to you just how meaningless passion can be."

He took her face in both hands while keeping his body pressed to hers, trapping her between himself and the tree. Not that she made any move to escape.

She stilled utterly, her eyes wide and dark as his head swept down and his mouth claimed her lips.

CHAPTER FOUR

Perhaps I can prove to you just how meaningless passion can be.

There was no time for the meaning of his words to sink in. There was only him. His hands holding her face, his mouth covering her own, the great length of his body sinking against her.

She froze in shock, horrified, confused . . . and admittedly thrilled.

Curtained in the shadow of dripping branches, the lightly pattering rain a distant drum in her ears, she could almost believe this was a dream. That Jamie, Owen's brother, had not backed her against a tree and covered her mouth with his ravaging lips, chasing the last bit of cold from her body. That it wasn't real. It was too delicious, too good to be real.

Before this moment, she had not permitted herself to acknowledge that he roused something within her. Perhaps she did not fully know it herself until this moment. With their first encounter, he had occupied her thoughts, but now she realized why.

This was desire.

He was the passion she'd been waiting for. The *more* . . .

Her hands hovered at her sides, unsure where to go. To shove him away? Or clutch him closer. Not that they could get any closer. She'd danced with gentlemen before, of course, but she'd never felt a man's body like this. So closely aligned with her own. The solid length of him, so strong and hard. Her kiss with Owen had been so sudden their bodies never even touched. Now, with Jamie . . . they touched everywhere. She imagined that she could feel the thump of his heart.

Her hands finally moved, drifted down to his shoulders. He tensed beneath her palms, his muscles bunching. A delicious heat swept through her.

His mouth wasn't tentative or gentle. He deepened the kiss, slanting his head to the side, taking her top lip between his, sucking, making her gasp. He took full advantage of her parted lips, sliding his tongue inside her mouth.

She jerked, tensing at the first stroke of his tongue against hers.

His mouth pulled back slightly, breathing husky words onto her lips. "Touch your tongue to mine."

Her belly clenched at his command. She complied, and his lips came over hers again, his open mouth hot and devouring, his tongue stroking hers again, coaxing a response.

She moved, tentative, uncertain, licking at his tongue once, twice.

He growled low in his throat with approval.

The sound emboldened her and she opened her mouth wider, copying the parries and thrusts of his tongue.

"That's it," he encouraged, his voice a rough rasp on her lips.

She rose on her tiptoes and pressed herself even closer. His fingers delved into her hair, loosening the knot and sending more tendrils falling around her face, tickling her cheeks and jaw.

She dug her fingers into his shoulders, tightening her grip as their kiss grew more intense. She moaned, pleasure eddying through her, pooling low in her belly and creating a tormenting ache.

He dragged a hand down the slick column of her throat, the rough pads of his fingers an erotic rasp against her wet flesh. His fingers clutched the edge of her bodice before delving in, the back of his fingers sliding deeply beneath the fabric, grazing the swell of her breast. Her heart constricted at the sensation of his fingers on her breast, edging a nipple.

Heat zinged through her from that sole contact, spreading to both breasts, tightening them until they almost hurt, throbbing for his touch.

She moaned and slid her arms around his neck, arching into his hand, yearning for more . . .

He answered her unspoken request. His mouth left hers and trailed down her throat. Each wet, open-mouthed kiss made her gasp and whimper, wiggle and writhe against him.

His hand tightened on both the corset and bodice of her gown, tugging them lower, as much as he could without ripping the fabric. Her breasts rose up, pushing free, the twin mounds exposed to the air, only a lacy chemise shielding them. Her skin puckered to gooseflesh in the cold. The chemise afforded little protection. He pulled loose the ribbon and then shoved the flimsy material aside. Her exposed nipples pinched and tightened in the frigid air.

She inhaled sharply, watching him cautiously, biting her lip in agony at the intense way he scrutinized her. His piercing gaze heightened everything inside her. The clench of her stomach muscles, the pull of her skin, the heavy ache of her breasts.

His hand glided over the sensitive mounds, warm palms brushing her nipples, back and forth, back and forth, sending the already hard tips into painfully tender peaks.

He lowered his head, watching her face as he did so, his sea-colored eyes gleaming with something akin to satisfaction—and something else she'd never seen before. Not directed at her at any rate. *Desire.*

Owen had never looked at her in such a way, which only seemed to confirm that he didn't feel for her what a man ought to feel for a woman he intended to marry. Perhaps it was not just her experiencing these doubts. Perhaps he did, as well.

A great sense of freedom seized her then, and at that exact moment Jamie's mouth closed over her. She cried out, arching into him as sucking, wet warmth enveloped her nipple. Her fingers dove into his damp hair, threading through the dark strands and clutching him close as his teeth grazed her. Her eyes widened, astonished at the splendid torment of his mouth.

"Oh," she said with a sigh, her eyes drifting shut.

"Open your eyes," he commanded.

She obeyed, glancing down at him gazing up at her. He looked positively seductive, his eyes hooded, inviting and knowing beneath dark lashes. Never removing his mouth from her, he played with the tip of her breast, his tongue stroking and tasting her.

She knew she should run. Should condemn him as wretched and amoral, but it was everything she had longed for without ever experiencing it previously. She'd longed for this. It was so much more, felt so much *better* than anything she had dreamed . . . Her imagination hadn't even touched on this. *But it was Jamie. His mouth. His hands.* Her mind shied away from the shocked whisper winding through her mind. She didn't want to think. She only wanted to *feel*.

She had wanted this. She had thrown the wish out there and he had answered it. At the moment, nothing else mattered. Not that this was Jamie, her childhood nemesis. Not that it was Owen's brother.

He turned his attention to her other breast and she moaned anew, her head falling back against the tree as his mouth pulled and sucked at her.

His hand swept around her back, gliding down her cloak, inching inexorably lower and landing expertly on her bottom. Cupping her with one hand, he lifted her against him, bringing her closer to the prod of his manhood. Even through her skirts, she felt it, she knew what it was, felt the evidence of his desire for her.

She felt a deep tug low in her belly. She squirmed closer, instinctively knowing, aching for the press of him against her. She lifted one leg, attempting to wrap it around him to get closer, to satisfy the desperate ache at her core.

He growled in approval and lifted his head from her breast and kissed her again. This time she had no hesitation. She met his lips, his tongue, with her own, took as much as she gave.

His hand curved under her thigh, supporting her leg as

he ground against her, rubbing himself at the juncture of her thighs where she burned and throbbed. She moaned into his mouth, the hard press of him against her exciting her more than she could stand.

"Jamie." She whimpered his name, a tiny, desperate mewl at the back of her throat. "Please." Her plea, her need for him, her need for more, was unmistakable even to her ears.

Gradually, he stilled against her. His mouth lifted. She chased after his lips with a small sound of distress, her hand skimming along his jaw as she tried to reclaim his mouth.

His body eased away and he released her thigh. Her leg slid back down to the ground slowly, shaking no matter how she tried to control it. He was withdrawing from her bit by bit.

"Paget," he said hoarsely. "We have to stop."

"Why?" She blinked up at him, focusing her hazy vision on his suddenly stern face. The locked jaw. The merciless eyes. No. She didn't want to see *that* Jamie again. She wanted the Jamie with heavy-lidded eyes and scalding lips.

"You belong to Owen. You always have."

The words struck her like a slap. "Why is everyone so certain of that?" She wanted to stomp her foot and throw back her head and shout.

"Why are you not? You love him. The two of you were inseparable. I well remember that. Neither of you had any interest in my existence."

There was something in his voice. Jealousy? Hurt? She didn't know if it had to do with her or his brother—perhaps both of them—but she heard it nonetheless. And she had a sudden image of him sitting astride his horse, watching as she and Owen scrambled up a tall rock wall that they were convinced he couldn't jump, hoping to avoid him. They had been children. Silly and thoughtless in their determination to leave him out. The memory shamed her now.

"I'm sorry," she murmured.

It was the wrong thing to say. She knew that at once. His eyes hardened. "Don't. Keep your pity."

"We weren't . . . very kind to you. I see that now." *See that you were lonely. That maybe you still are . . .*

"Stop," he growled. "Don't. This is not about me."

But she wanted it to be about him. And her. *Them.*

She sighed and reached for him. "I don't want to talk about Owen anymore." She supposed she sounded wretched saying so, but staring at Jamie she only wanted more. More of him. More of the desire he'd just shown her. It was like waking up to a whole new world of colors.

As though he could read the desperate hunger in her face, he stepped back two paces, leaving her cold and alone against the tree. Reality slowly descended. His gaze slid down to her chest. She glanced down, remembering herself, mortified to see her breasts, the skin pink from his thorough attentions, exposed to the elements and his gaze. Those hard eyes sparked for a moment before sharply glancing away.

"Cover yourself," he said tersely. As though he had not been the one to start this little lesson in passion and unclothe her in the first place.

Her trembling fingers fumbled with the loosened ribbons of her chemise. Even as she worked quickly, tugging her corset and gown back into place, her chin jerked high, pride stiffening her spine. She refused to let him shame her. She'd behaved no more scandalously than he.

Finished arranging her clothing, she pulled her cloak tighter around her, grateful for the additional barrier. Still, when he returned his searing stare to her, she found it wasn't enough. After what had just transpired between them, she doubted if she would ever feel anything other than vulnerable around him again.

A long moment passed, and he said nothing. Her fingers clenched around the edges of her cloak until they ached bone-deep. At last he announced grimly, dispassionately, "And that's how meaningless desire can be."

Understanding dawned as his words sank in.

He had used her to prove a point.

He had manipulated her with the very thing she craved.

She'd never felt so . . . *small*. So foolish.

Her palm itched to slap him, but she refused to permit herself to do that again. She curled her fingers into a fist, resisting the impulse. He deserved it, but she would not show how much he had affected her. "You *are* worse than I remembered."

She squeezed past him and put several paces between them, giving him a wide berth. He rotated, watching her impassively. There was nothing in his eyes, and it became clear to her that what they had just shared had meant nothing. Just as he claimed.

His earlier words now echoed through her: *Perhaps I can prove to you just how meaningless passion can be.* He had succeeded in that. In fact, he had made it abundantly clear how meaningless passion could be. For some people. *For him.* Disappointment cut her as keenly as a knife's blade.

Tiny prickles of heat washed over her face and neck as she

thought of all that had passed between them ... all she had allowed him to do, all she had *reveled* in.

It had been nothing, an experiment for him. A lesson he had sought to teach her.

And teach me he had. He had her panting and begging for his touch, his mouth, him, against that tree. And it meant nothing. Less than nothing.

Presenting him with her back, she walked away, clutching her cloak to her throat, clinging to the frayed edges of her dignity, refusing to let him crush that, too.

Jamie watched her go, the memory of her dark eyes flashing with a mixture of hurt and rage imprinted on his mind. It only made her more appealing, her eyes more luminous—and made him feel that much more a bastard.

He'd chosen his words carefully, determined to make his point ... determined to guarantee that she despise him ... that she forget about giving up on Owen and her foolish quest for a marriage of passion.

It didn't matter that his words were a lie.

From the first touch, the first taste of her mouth, he'd wanted to lose himself inside her. Consume every inch of her until they were both thoroughly spent. He had not anticipated such a reaction. He had not thought matters would spiral so quickly out of his control. He dragged a shaking hand through his wet hair. That had been more than the kiss he planned. *You practically had your way with her against a tree.*

Nothing about what just occurred was meaningless to him. He was relieved she did not realize the lie of his words. As a girl, her bold gaze had always managed to see straight through him. She'd frightened him a bit then. And to be honest, she still did. There was nothing half measure about her.

He rubbed the back of his knuckles against his lips. He could still taste her. She was the type of female men lived and died for. His body still hummed, aching for her—her lips, her skin, her breasts . . .

Owen—he quickly supplanted. She was the type of woman Owen lived and died for. Not him.

He imagined Owen somewhere in barren terrain. He well remembered the heat, the bugs that gnawed on flesh. The death. The blood. He winced to think of how he had just very nearly ravished Paget. The only thing Owen had was the lure of home. Memories of this place and Paget. He'd not steal that from him. She would be waiting for him when he returned.

He watched as her cloaked figure grew smaller and smaller.

He would do the right thing. Perhaps for the first time in his life. He would be a good brother and not think about the loneliness of his own life and all that he didn't have. It was not Owen's fault that their father had favored him . . . that Brand had favored him . . . that Paget belonged to him.

He would cease begrudging his brother, cease coveting what was his. Jamie would resist Paget. He would do the right thing. No matter what Paget awoke inside him. No matter that he wanted her.

CHAPTER FIVE

"Paget, are you paying attention? Honestly, you've been wool-gathering all morning. How am I ever to finish these love knots in time?" Alice Mary stared at her expectantly. *Accusingly.*

Paget snapped her attention to the mounds of pink and yellow ribbon spread out in front of her. Her fingers fever-ishly resumed working.

"I'm sorry, Alice Mary." Her cheeks burned at the direc-tion of her wayward thoughts. She had been reliving yester-day. *Again.* It was bad enough she had stayed awake all night thinking of Jamie. His mouth on her. His hands. *His mouth.* She couldn't shake the memories. Not even after the callous way he had treated her. It was as though the way he made her feel superseded anything he said.

She threaded the pink and yellow ribbons through her fingers into loops. Alice Mary wanted the love knots to hang suspended from the ceiling. An ambitious plan with the ball only four days away. "How many more do we need?" At least fifty sat piled high on a nearby table, the work of Paget and Alice Mary.

Alice Mary tsked her tongue and went back to counting. "We need at least a hundred more. Don't you remember me telling you? Really, Paget, you're about as distracted as I was when I first met my John." Her hands froze. She dropped a half-formed love knot into her lap, heedless that she hadn't even tied it off yet. "Paget Ellsworth, are you besotted?"

"Don't be silly!" Even as she protested, heat crept over her face and she stared with renewed fascination at the ribbon in her hands.

"You're blushing. It's true," Alice Mary declared with relish. "There is someone." She moved to drop down beside Paget on the settee she occupied, heedless that she sat upon several yards of ribbons *and* Paget's skirts.

Paget gave her skirts a helpless tug. She was well and truly trapped.

"There's no one," she insisted.

Alice Mary watched her with narrow eyes, contemplating. "Indeed," she mused. "Everyone always assumed that you and Owen would marry. But he has been gone so dreadfully long, has he not?" A long pause followed this.

Paget slid her a wary glance. "Er, yes. He has."

"You know what they say?" Alice Mary added.

Paget rose to the bait. She could not help herself. "What do they say?"

She waved a hand airily. "Oh, about absence making the heart forgetful."

Paget frowned. "I think you have that in the reverse."

"Do I?" Alice Mary angled her head. "Well, no mind. My point is this—" She leveled a serious look at Paget. "I for one never thought you and Owen were fated. Not as everyone else."

Paget blinked and sat up straighter. "No? That certainly puts you in the minority. Why did you never tell me before?"

Alice Mary shrugged one shoulder. "I figured you would realize it for yourself, but then he went away to war, and you've formed no other attachments. I fear that obligation to Owen holds you in check."

Immediately, Jamie's face flashed before her. Evidently she was not in check. Not at all.

"You don't think it wretched of me?" She moistened her lips. "I mean how will Owen feel if he returns to find me and someone else—"

Alice Mary covered her hand with her own. "You cannot prevent yourself from living for fear of hurting Owen's feelings. I'm sure he only wants you happy. No one would blame you for seeking out your own happiness. Not even him."

She winced. "I'm not so certain of that." She could think of one person who would blame her if she sought her own happiness. He would *heartily* blame her.

"There was never that spark between the two of you." Alice Mary nodded almost sadly. "I watched you both together and always thought you behaved more like friends than sweethearts."

Paget nodded, understanding perfectly now that she'd sampled the spark firsthand. "I confess that I've come to think the same thing myself."

"Ah-ha!" Alice Mary's eyes danced with delight. "So there *is* someone. Hm." She tapped her chin. "Who could it be? He'd have to be young . . ."

"No," Paget quickly rejoined. "There is no one." The last thing she wanted was for her friend to start wondering thoughts that led her to conclude that the Earl of Winningham had struck her fancy. "Only I'm open to the possibility of forming an attachment to an eligible gentleman. That is all."

Alice Mary clapped her hands together gleefully, her blue eyes glinting conspiratorially. "Well! Then we shall endeavor to find you a worthy gentleman who can deliver a spark. My ball shall be the perfect place to start. Let me think. An old school friend of John's will be attending. Mr. Bromley is quite the gentleman. He cuts a fine figure. I've witnessed many a lady bat her fan in his direction. And what better setting than a Valentine's ball to set the stage for romance? If my efforts come to no avail, Cupid will surely have a hand in this."

Paget smiled and hoped it looked sincere and not as brittle as it felt.

Somehow after yesterday's kiss—*kisses*—very well, it was rather more than a simple kiss. Her face heated as she thought of all the wicked things his mouth did to her—it felt false to forge a romance with someone else so soon. To feel passion again in such a short amount of time. Surely passion wasn't that easy? Surely it wasn't something to be had with just anyone?

If that were the case, she would have had it with Owen. That would have been preferable. Instead her body had reacted and chosen Jamie.

She scowled at the turn of her thoughts. It almost sounded as though she felt loyal toward Jamie. Absurd. He certainly felt no fondness for her.

But she refused to let him ruin her dream.

Her smile widened. Perhaps a Valentine's ball *would* be

the perfect place to begin the romance she so desperately craved.

She nodded and smiled at Alice Mary. "I should be delighted to meet your Mr. Bromley."

Jamie strolled amid the partygoers, edging the dance floor where hundreds of delicate love knots dangled from ribbons attached to the ceiling. The baroness had obviously gone to great efforts for tonight's ball.

He stopped to greet familiar faces as he scanned the crush, straining for a glimpse of Paget. He hadn't seen her since their encounter in the rain. He imagined there would be some awkwardness. Especially on her part. No doubt she would not even be able to meet his gaze. Despite her bold manner, she was a country miss. A vicar's daughter. Inexperienced. She was probably mortified, hiding behind a potted fern hoping to avoid him.

For the best, he supposed. Especially considering he'd thought of little else besides her. Her scent. Her taste. It was utter torment. Although worth it if he had succeeded in securing her for Owen. That's all that mattered. Not her discomfort. Not his.

His smile grew pained. He wasn't one to endure idle banter. Meaningless chatter was simply that to him. Meaningless. He would typically have avoided a fête like this. He always had before. As a boy. As a young man. He'd never felt at ease in these gatherings. He was not like Brand or Owen, so at ease and free with a quip.

But he was the earl now, and a voice inside him had

prompted him to attend and be more sociable. More like his father and brothers. Beloved among the villagers and local gentry. The kind of lord who took his station seriously, who embraced the responsibility of his role and fraternized with the people under his care. The kind of earl even Owen would be if he was the heir. Perhaps, in the back of his mind, he thought his father might be looking down on him now.

He winced. Still chasing after his approval it would seem.

He nodded at a widow, garbed from head to foot in starched bombazine, whose name he couldn't recall. She prattled on, sharing some anecdote about his father.

He gulped down the last of his champagne, wishing for something stronger.

"Oh, it's splendid having you home safely, my lord. We're all praying for the safe return of your brother."

"You're too kind," he murmured.

"Nonsense. Lord McDowell is loved by all. We can't lose him, too."

"I am sure he will return safely."

Suddenly he caught a glimpse of hair as pale as moonbeams. It was there for a second and then gone, lost amid dancing figures and fluttering love knots.

He set his glass down. "If you'll pardon me," he murmured, not even hearing the widow's response as he walked along the perimeter of the dance floor, stalking only one female.

He saw nothing else, acknowledged no one, nor the stares he was getting as he chased after another glimpse of the hair that could belong to only one. Suddenly bodies parted and there was a break in the crowd.

And there she was.

Fetching in a white gown trimmed in pink and gold ribbon. The waltz faded to a close and she stepped free of her partner's arms.

Jamie inched along, watching as the pair glided together from the dance floor. Her partner settled her hand in the crook of his arm much too intimately in Jamie's opinion. She glowed, her face flushed and her dark eyes gleaming like polished onyx.

A foul taste coated his mouth as the fair-haired man at her side closed his hand over hers in the crook of her arm. Who was he? Had she already moved on, found a suitor to deliver on the passion she sought? Apparently his actions hadn't frightened her from her selfish quest, after all. A growl rose up in his throat as he watched them move toward the balcony door.

"Lord Winningham, so delighted you could attend our little fête this evening."

He turned his gaze to the baroness, detecting the barest hint of scorn in her gaze. No one else would note it, but he did. Although all politeness, he detected the chilly reserve in her blue eyes. She'd never cared for him. Of course not. She was a friend to Paget and probably knew every wretched thing he had ever done or said.

"I wouldn't miss it," he returned, performing a quick bow over her hand and donning an affable smile.

"Indeed." Her smile deepened but still did not quite reach her eyes.

He could not help himself; his gaze slid to the balcony doors just as Paget and the stranger reached them.

"Have you made the acquaintance of Mr. Bromley yet? Such a delightful man."

He shot her a quick glance, seeing she had followed his gaze to the departing pair.

"No, I have not had the pleasure."

"Mr. Bromley attended school with my dear Sir John."

There was something in her voice that snared his attention. A certain wistfulness. He looked at her again. Even though Paget and the gentleman in question had vanished outdoors, the baroness still stared after them, a vaguely cunning look on her face.

Watching her closely, he murmured, "Unfortunate he does not live in closer proximity."

She looked back at him. "He's close enough. Relationships have been forged with greater distances as a hurdle."

And with that, he knew. She was matchmaking Paget with this Bromley fellow. He inhaled deeply, his chest tightening uncomfortably.

From all appearances, Paget had no intention on waiting for Owen. She had made up her mind. She was actively searching for her *passionate* romance. Anger simmered in his veins. Apparently she had found her first candidate in Bromley.

He clung to his smile and murmured, "I understand completely. And so would my brother, Lord McDowell." He let his gaze settle on her pointedly. "He would agree with you that relationships can stand the test of any distance. And time."

Faint color spotted her cheeks. It gratified him to see that she was not without conscience. She might not care for him, but he knew she cared about his brother. She should consider Owen as she was thrusting Paget into the arms of other men. His hand curled at his side at the mere notion.

"Indeed," she muttered. Looking over her shoulder, she feigned an expression of distraction . . . as though suddenly seeing something that required her attention. "If you'll pardon me, my lord."

"Of course." He wasted little time watching her weave through the crowd. He cut a line straight for the balcony doors, intent on locating Paget and putting a stop to her budding romance with Bromley. For Owen. He owed it to Owen.

It had nothing to do with the hot surge of possession that rose up inside him at the thought of Paget in the arms of another man.

CHAPTER SIX

Several guests milled along the stretch of balcony, reassuring Paget that a stroll with her dancing partner was not unseemly. Flushed from dancing, Paget didn't even mind the chill.

"You dance like an angel, Miss Ellsworth."

Paget stifled a snort at the compliment. An exaggeration to say the least, but she was flattered nonetheless. Jamie would never bother to praise her with such a falsehood. He wasn't the sort to issue empty praise. At least he wouldn't waste his breath doing so to *her*. On the other hand, perhaps a lady he was courting . . .

Blast! Must he her thoughts turn to him at every turn?

She slid her companion a glance beneath her lashes as he led her down the steps toward the burbling fountain. A self-proclaimed outdoorsman, Bromley was handsome and ruddy-faced from long hours outside. Only a few inches taller than herself, he was stocky and solid enough to make her feel feminine beside him despite his lack of height.

They circled the fountain, her hand snug in the crook of

his arm. "You're not cold?" he inquired. "I could fetch your cloak for you."

She shook her head. "Thank you, no. The dancing left me quite warm."

He nodded agreeably. "Dancing can be exerting, as well as diverting. An excellent recreation."

She nodded, too, wondering if they should move on to the topic of weather next. She bit the inside of her cheek and reprimanded herself to give him a chance. He could simply be nervous and not merely boring. She needed to be more amenable. Every other male in the vicinity considered her unavailable. He was the first gentleman whom she had not known all her life who actually appeared interested in her.

Fewer people mingled around the fountain, so close to the spray of the water. Paget and Bromley rounded the backside of it, well out of sight of any guests.

"I confess to apprehension when the baroness insisted that we meet."

Paget laughed lightly. "She is not known for her subtly."

"In this case, I am only glad at her enthusiasm."

Her gaze flicked to his lips. Nice enough, she supposed. She wondered if they possessed the power to reduce her to a quivering state of desire as Jamie's mouth had done.

Devil it! There she went again, consumed with thoughts of him, comparing the first gentleman she met to him.

He turned and caught her staring so intently at him. She knew modesty should dictate that she look away . . . for her to behave as a demure vicar's daughter ought to in the company of a gentleman she only just met. And yet she couldn't do that. She was too curious. Too determined to see if what had transpired with her and Jamie had truly been a singular event.

His look turned speculative as he held her gaze.

Clearing his throat, he turned away for a moment, scanning the area around them, confirming that they were in fact alone.

Satisfied, he inched ever closer. "Miss Ellsworth," he murmured. "Is it rash of me to say how propitious I find our meeting this evening?"

She smiled, trying to ignore her frisson of unease as the front of his jacket brushed against her. How would she know if what she experienced with Jamie was a truly singular occurrence if she did not . . . *practice* with other gentlemen?

He reached a hand to her cheek and brushed back a loose tendril of hair. "I owe a debt to our hostess."

His eyes were close now, and she could see, even in the dim shadows, that they were quite brown. Dull and lightless.

She was suddenly filled with the certainty that he was going to kiss her. His face inched closer, moving slowly, testing her willingness, giving her plenty of time to pull away. But why should she do that? She had begun this.

Except now, kissing this man, this stranger—on the heel of Jamie's kiss—struck her as thoroughly distasteful. Drat the man! He was ruining matters even when he was not present to do so.

She flattened a hand on Mr. Bromley's chest, ready to push him away, when a deep voice cut through the evening.

"Ah, there you are."

Mr. Bromley jumped and took a hasty step back.

Her face flushed guiltily, imagining how they must look. Her gaze swung to the new arrival and her stomach sank. She should have known that voice. It haunted her thoughts since his return.

Mr. Bromley blinked, stiffening. "Begging your pardon—"

"Lord Winningham," she murmured, her voice breathless.

Mr. Bromley relaxed at the sound of Jamie's title and smoothed a hand along the nonexistent wrinkles marring the front of his jacket, suddenly mindful of his appearance. He took an even wider step from her, putting a respectable distance between them.

"You must be Mr. Bromley. One of the ladies . . ." He tapped his chin looking insincerely apologetic. "Sorry. I've forgotten her name. Been gone too long, I fear. She asked me to fetch you."

Forgot her name indeed! Paget would wager that there was no such lady in need of Mr. Bromley. Her gaze narrowed on Jamie.

"I suppose I best return inside. Miss Ellsworth?" Mr. Bromley looked at her uncertainly, regretfully.

"I'll see her back," Jamie volunteered.

Bromley nodded and executed a quick bow before hurrying away.

"That was dreadful of you," she charged as soon as they were alone.

"I did what needed to be done to save you from yourself."

"I was not aware that I was in need of saving."

"Come. You did not think to toss Owen aside for *that?*" He waved a hand in the direction Mr. Bromley had taken.

She lifted her nose. "Mr. Bromley is a gentleman."

"A gentleman." He snorted. "I thought you were looking for passion. You'll hardly find it with the likes of him. You could do better."

"Forgive me if I don't trust your advice, my lord."

He shrugged. "I simply can't see that prig giving you a taste of what you so obviously crave."

Her cheeks burned. "You make it sound so terribly vulgar."

His eyes peered at her, dark in the shadows of the garden. "Have you forgotten what transpired between us? I haven't. I know what burns inside you." He stepped closer, his voice lowering to a husky pitch. "I tasted it for myself." He motioned behind him. "When it comes to what you're looking for, you won't find it in any of the gentlemen in that ballroom."

Her breath caught. "You're saying you are not like them then?" She meant to trap him into admitting he was not a gentleman.

"I am not," he rejoined, not appearing to care at the admission. "Not in the least." His gaze crawled over her face. "If I were a gentleman I wouldn't still be here with you." His hand lifted to her face. She waited, the air trapped tightly in her chest. "I would have fled as soon as I broke up your little rendezvous with Bromley. But I'm still here. Near you. Touching you."

His fingers landed on her mouth then, tracing their contours, lightly grazing the sensitive flesh. His voice continued, rolling through her like honey. "Feeling this mouth. Remembering your taste."

She sighed against his fingers. If he meant to torment her, he was succeeding. Her heart beat as fierce as a rabbit's beneath her breastbone.

"Please," she begged.

"Please what?" he demanded, his voice hard for all its softness.

"Kiss me again."

It was as though he'd been waiting for just that invitation. He hauled her into his arms and claimed her mouth.

Tongue tangling with hers, his fingers slid into her hair, scattering the pins. She didn't even let herself care how she would repair her simple coiffure. There was only his mouth. On hers. His body against hers.

A lick of heat curled low in her belly, tightening and twisting until she grew wet between the legs. His hands slid lower, his fingers digging into her back.

She moaned into his mouth, hating the clothing barring them from each other. She wanted to go back to that day with him in the rain and feel his hands on her naked flesh. His mouth on her bared breasts. She wanted that and more. She wanted all their clothes gone until they were nothing but skin on skin.

Pressing herself against him, she wound her arms around his neck, marveling at the insistent ache throbbing at her core.

Her fingers wove through his hair, luxuriating in the softness, in her freedom to touch him as he touched her.

His hands slid down to her derrière. She felt boneless, ready to melt. Her fingers clutched his jacket as if that was all that kept her from sliding to the ground. Their lips clung, drinking, tasting, devouring each other. With a growl, he wrenched his lips from hers, dragging his mouth down the column of her throat, sucking, nipping at the cords along her neck. Her head fell back, granting him greater access.

His hold tightened, his breath firing against her throat. She opened her eyes to see his gleaming at her in the gloom of the garden, as though lit from within. She tugged him by the head, bringing his lips back to hers.

Dimly, in the back of her mind that was not overrun with sensation, she heard voices growing louder. The tread of footsteps on the path registered too late. Almost simultaneously she heard a sharp gasp.

She shoved at Jamie's chest and jerked back a stumbling step.

Her horrified gaze moved from his face to scan the garden. She spotted them immediately. Her eyes closed in a long, anguished blink. Of all people, Mrs. Willoughby and Miss Manchester were the worst. The widow and her spinster sister weren't simply gossips. They lived vicariously through the lives of others. Everything must be discussed again and again for the full effect, even when the news was weeks old.

The ladies clung to each other, squeezing each other's hands as if they stood witness to some terrible debacle and not a mere kiss. Their mouths sagged, heightening their resemblance to each other.

"Mrs. Willoughby, Miss Manchester," she greeted with enough cheer to make her wince.

"Miss Ellsworth," Mrs. Willoughby cried in a voice full of affront and, if Paget's ears were not mistaken, a healthy dose of glee.

"Oh, forgive us . . ." Paget glanced at Jamie. His expression was impassive. She frowned, hoping he would say something, *do* something.

She looked helplessly back to the sisters, telling herself that this wasn't as damaging as she first feared. A single kiss wasn't ruinous. It was not as though they had seen her with her dress pulled down and Jamie lavishing his mouth on her breasts. *That* would have been ruinous. Not this . . . surely . . . not . . .

"Lord Winningham and I were simply sharing a brief, friendly kiss . . . to welcome him home . . ." Her cheeks heated at her outrageous words. She did not need to see their incredulous expressions to know just how very lame that excuse rang.

There had been nothing innocent about their kiss. Staring at the women, she knew they did not for one moment consider it an innocent peck either. They knew it for exactly what it had been . . . a passionate, hungry kiss.

"Indeed," Mrs. Willoughby said haughtily. "That is some welcome home kiss. I cannot even imagine how you shall greet Lord McDowell upon his return."

Miss Manchester tittered. "Let us hope there are no prying eyes to that auspicious event."

The reminder of Owen made her face burn. Of course, they believed her to be a faithless harlot . . . kissing his older brother whilst he fought for their country legions away.

She wanted to stamp her foot in frustration. She did not belong to Owen. She was a free woman . . . entitled to kiss whom she chose.

"Well, pardon us, we have no wish to intrude further." Miss Manchester nodded to each of them and tugged on her sister's arm, pulling her back down the path toward the house.

Once they were out of sight, she whirled on Jamie. "A great deal of help you were!" she charged.

He shrugged. "What could I say? There was no erasing what they witnessed."

"Brilliant! Now every tongue will be wagging that I

kissed *you* ... Owen's brother!" She groaned, waving her arms wildly.

He nodded grimly. "I'll speak with your father tomorrow."

She stilled, dropping her arms at her sides. "Whatever for?"

He sighed heavily. "Do I need to say it? There is but one recourse here."

She shook her head blankly, utterly befuddled.

He pointed in the direction Miss Manchester and Mrs. Willoughby fled. "Those two biddies are at this very moment regaling all who will listen with the news that I have thoroughly compromised you."

She jerked back as though slapped. "Compromised? I would not go so far as to say that—"

"No? Even now wagers are being made on how long until it becomes evident you are 'increasing.'"

She gasped. "Of all the vulgar—"

" 'Tis the truth. You are compromised, Paget. There is only one thing left for us to do."

"Marriage?" She choked the word out as if it were the foulest of epithets.

He nodded, his mouth pulling in a tight frown. Clearly, he was no more thrilled at the prospect than she.

She stared at his impassive face, searching for some sign that he was hesitant on the matter. He was quite serious. "What of Owen? I thought I was to wait for Owen? You seemed quite adamant on that point."

"It's too late to worry for Owen. I must protect you now." His lips twisted sardonically. "Owen would expect that of me."

She shook her head. "You make no sense."

"It's simple. Either I leave you in scandal, utterly and irreparably ruined. Or I save your name and wed you. Neither situation will please my brother, but even he would agree that the former is unacceptable. The latter, a lesser evil, if you will."

She blinked. "You just characterized marriage to me as an evil?

He winced. "That's not precisely what I meant to say, Paget."

She wasn't too sure about that. Everything about him was dour and disappointed. He clearly did not *want* to marry her. Obligation drove him and nothing else. Oh, how he would come to resent her if she agreed. And if it cost him a relationship with his brother, he might grow to loathe her. No matter that he had been just as much a participant in that kiss. He would look at her and see only what she had cost him. His freedom. His brother. She could not live with that.

Shaking her head, she began to turn away. "No. No. This cannot be happening. I won't do this . . ."

He followed her and seized her arm, forcing her to turn and face him. "This affects not only you—"

"Oh. It damages *you*, does it?" She snorted her skepticism. "I don't see how. You're a man. An earl. You can ruin girls up and down the countryside and your reputation shall remain intact." A bitter truth that only increased her fury at the helpless situation she suddenly found herself in. She twisted her arm free of his grip. "Thank you for the offer to sacrifice yourself, but I shall weather the storm on my own."

"I'm not speaking of me."

"No? Who then?"

"Your father," he bit out. "Do you really think he can survive the scandal?"

She sucked in a breath. Suddenly she felt both hot and cold.

He continued, "Think about it, Paget. His flock would desert him."

All because of her.

"Oh," she expelled the word on a sigh as she visualized the scenario he was describing. Misery filled her heart. He was right. This could destroy Papa.

How was it possible for wild and exciting sensations to have consumed her only moments before? The euphoria she felt in his arms felt like a distant thing as anguish filled her heart.

He released her, his stormy blue-green eyes waiting.

It didn't matter if she fled anymore. There was no running away from it. He released her.

Her eyes stung as she gazed up at him. "It's not supposed to be like this."

"What's not?" he queried, angling his head.

Her proposal. *Marriage.* She wasn't supposed to wed someone out of obligation and necessity. She wanted . . . *more.*

She bit back the words from tumbling free. He already knew as much. She felt as fragile as glass at the moment. She could not abide it if he mocked her.

And that's when she realized she had been fooling herself. It wasn't just passion she wanted. She wanted love. That was the elusive *more* she had been craving.

Staring into Jamie's grim face, she was reminded of the stern and humorless boy he had been. She wanted love and she would never have that from this man.

Swallowing back a choked sob, she turned and fled

through the back of the garden. Nothing on earth would have her brave the ballroom now. She'd circle around to the front and have a footman fetch Papa for her.

Perhaps once she was home she could figure a way out of this mess. Perhaps it wasn't nearly as bad as Jamie seemed to think it would be. Perhaps she would be able to laugh about this a fortnight from now.

As she rounded to the front of the house, her father was already waiting outside beside their carriage, her cloak in his hands, his shoulders hunkered in a way she had never seen before. Usually Papa stood tall and proud, his shoulders pulled back. Suddenly he looked older. Frail.

Her steps slowed as she approached, dread sinking its teeth deep into her heart as she read his expression.

He held out a hand to her. "Come, daughter. Let us go home."

A thick lump formed in her throat. Nodding, she placed her hand in her father's and allowed him to assist her inside the carriage.

There would be no future laughter about this night.

A hushed silence fell once they settled inside the carriage.

"Daughter," Papa began.

Heat filled her cheeks. She blinked stinging eyes, hating that she had shamed her father. He was everything to her since her mother had died. She could not bear the thought that she had disappointed him.

"I'm sorry, Papa," she murmured.

He patted her hand. "Fret not. I was young once. And in love." His eyes twinkled at her through the lenses of his spectacles, smudged as always from his fingerprints.

She sniffed and rubbed the cold tip of her nose. "I cannot blame my behavior on that sentiment."

"No? You do not love him then?"

She shook her head. "I—I don't know." She knew she felt something for him. Perhaps it was love. It couldn't simply be lust. Although there was that. In abundance. Her body grew warm, her bones liquefying just thinking about him . . . his mouth . . . his hands. But love? Something lasting and deep?

Whatever she felt started when he showed her that glimpse of himself . . . the lonely boy he had been, looking with longing after her and Owen. He'd had no one. No friends that she could recall. His brothers preferred the company of each other . . . of *her*. That must have stung. Even his father seemed quite unaffected by his existence. As if he didn't care one way or another if Jamie lived or died. Harsh, perhaps, but not untrue.

She knew the late Earl of Winningham had been exceedingly proud of Brand, his heir, taking him about the countryside and showing him the proper manner in which to oversee his holdings and attend those dependent on him. Owen had been favored as well, the son of his second wife, a Scottish countess whom he had doted upon.

Only now did she realize Jamie had been overlooked . . . and left alone.

She understood loneliness. Since Owen left her, she had been lonely. Living, going about her days, but without feeling anything. Bored. Numb. Jamie had changed all that the moment he returned. She was alive again. He'd brought her back to life.

Papa sighed. "I'm certain the earl will attempt to set matters to rights and offer marriage."

She nodded, staring at her hands. "He has."

"Paget, listen well ... you needn't make any decisions until you *do* know your heart."

Paget snapped her attention back to her father. "I do not think I have that luxury."

He patted her hand again. "You take all the time you need. Marriage is not a decision to be made lightly. It is the rest of your life you are deciding."

"Papa, this affects you, too."

"Don't fret about me." He smiled. "Do I look worried?"

She smiled hesitantly. "No."

"Then you shouldn't give me another thought. Look inside her your heart. Then go from there." He slid his hand from hers and turned to stare out the window, looking quite at peace.

She wished she felt half as content.

CHAPTER SEVEN

Jamie arrived at the vicarage at first light. He'd debated following Paget home the previous evening but thought it best to give her the night to gather her thoughts and adjust to the reality of her situation. Their situation, he amended, his jaw clenching.

He'd done this to the both of them. No mistake about it. And it had nothing to do with his need to protect his brother. He'd been selfish and greedy for her. Kissing Paget again had been totally self-driven, and the consequences were his to bear. Owen would never forgive him, but there was no way around it. He could not stand aside and watch as Paget fell to ruin. The least he could do was not openly *enjoy* the notion that she would be his . . . that he could have her in his bed. He could reach for her any time. Touch her. Kiss her. Sink inside her body and spend himself.

Amazingly, in the span of one night, he had grown to accept the idea. Even anticipate it. Almost like it was always meant to be. Paget and him. Not Paget and Owen.

The housekeeper led him to Vicar Ellsworth's office.

He waited only moments in the small space before the vicar joined him.

"Lord Winningham," he greeted, moving before the crackling fireplace where Jamie stood warming his hands. He motioned for Jamie to seat himself in one of the wingback chairs. "I was hoping you would call."

"Of course. I would not be remiss with my duty."

The vicar lowered into the chair across from him. Despite his much shorter frame, he managed to look down his spectacles at Jamie. "Duty? Is that what brings you here?"

"I apologize for putting Paget's reputation at risk. It was not my intention—"

"What was your intention, Lord Winningham?"

Jamie blinked, unsure how to respond to that bald question. How could he admit that he had not thought much beyond getting his hands on Paget? Touching her, kissing her, tasting her? He certainly couldn't admit such a thing to her father—a bloody vicar, no less.

"I will not leave Paget to weather this. Naturally, I've come to offer marriage."

The vicar studied him thoughtfully for several moments. "I appreciate your sense of responsibility, my lord. Very honorable. But I'm afraid that is not enough for my daughter."

Jamie jerked slightly, certain he had misunderstood. "Begging your pardon, sir, but you are denying my suit?"

The vicar nodded. "I've always thought my daughter's heart was bound to your brother."

A growl rose up in his throat. For the first time, he felt a surge of violence toward his absent brother. Since the last night, he had grown quite accustomed, even gratified, with the notion that Paget was his now. He squashed the sentiment, disgusted himself for it.

"Have you asked your daughter? I think she would tell you that her heart is quite unattached when it comes to my brother—"

"I've come to gather that." He nodded, pushing his slipping spectacles back up his nose. "I'll grant you that she wouldn't be so susceptible to your . . . charms if her heart were engaged with your brother."

He sighed, relieved he did not have to persuade the vicar that Paget was not bound to Owen.

"That said, it's *your* heart that concerns me."

"My heart?"

"Yes. I'm not convinced your affections for my daughter run deep enough."

He stared at the vicar, quite dumbfounded. "You realize I compromised your daughter. You both stand to become social pariahs? Your very livelihood could be threatened. Even with my support, empty pews on Sunday would be harmful to your position here."

The vicar nodded. "Yes. That would be a shame, but there are greater tragedies in life."

Jamie stared at him blankly. "Such as . . ."

The vicar continued, "Such as finding yourself married to someone for whom you feel nothing more than a fleeting attraction. The desires of the flesh are ephemeral. Only love lasts."

He opened his mouth to object, but could not find the words to persuade the vicar, short of claiming he was in love with Paget. His throat tightened as the very possibility seized him. In love? With Paget? Could it be? The image of her filled his mind and his palms prickled with the overwhelming urge to find her. Hold her close until her father approved of his suit.

He visualized her perfectly. Heard the echo of her voice in his mind. *I want passion. Desire.* She had no qualms, no shame, admitting it to him. Like a siren's call, her request was something he'd been unable to ignore. Even if she had not issued it directly to him. And yet she wanted more than that. She wanted it all. Everything. Passion wrapped up in love. The most alarming thing of all was that he couldn't help thinking loving her would be the easiest thing in the world to do.

Perhaps he already did. Clawing panic swept over him. How could he let that happen? He'd never been good enough. Not even for his own family. What made him think she wanted his love?

Vicar Ellsworth stared at him as if waiting for his admission of love. When it didn't arrive, the older gentleman stood. "Thank you for calling. I feel much better now that we've had this talk." The vicar smiled as if he had not just denied the earl's offer of marriage.

Feeling as though he had failed some sort of test, Jamie allowed himself to be led from the office. Upon departing the house, he stopped in the yard and turned. A flicker of curtains in an upstairs window caught his notice. He thought he saw a flash of pale, moonbeam hair.

His panic evaporated. The vague, unsettled feeling lifted from his chest. Resolve stole over him. He felt as though he were back in India, with fresh orders in his hands and a mission to complete.

He had not failed. This was not over.

He and Paget were not even close to being finished.

Paget lurched up in bed with a gasp, her eyes searching the gloom. The remnants of a dream clung like shadowy cobwebs. She clutched the counterpane and pulled it high to her chest. The wind howled outside her window, rattling the panes.

She'd been on a battlefield, searching for Owen. She called his name again and again, pushing through the smoke, walking amid fallen soldiers. At last she'd come to him. *Alive!* She embraced him, holding tightly. He set her from him, looking at her sternly.

"Find Jamie, Paget."

"Jamie?" She glanced around at the carnage, her heart constricting. "He's here?"

Owen nodded. "Of course, he's here. He's always been here. Only you can find him."

Nodding, she staggered from Owen's side, calling for Jamie. Holding her skirts to keep from tripping, she hunted for him among the mayhem. Then she spotted him on a distant rise. She rushed to reach him, Owen's words playing in her mind. *Only you can find him. He's always been here.*

Just as she was about to reach him, a blast of artillery shook the earth, launching her through the air. She landed on her back, gasping for breath. Rolling to her side, she looked to where she'd last seen Jamie. Only burning, smoldering earth remained. Staggering to her feet, she screamed for him, but he was gone.

Her breath fell in hard pants as if she were still on that

battlefield, hunting for Jamie. She rubbed her hands over her face, wondering what it all meant.

"Just a dream," she whispered to herself, shaking off the cobwebs of slumber. Still, she couldn't slow her heartbeat.

Her window rattled louder. She frowned and shoved back the covers. Swinging her legs over the side, her bare feet dropped down silently. Rising, she moved toward the window. Pulling back the curtains, she almost screamed at the sight of Jamie, perched in a tree, knuckles rapping the glass.

She quickly unlatched the window and stepped back, watching in astonishment as Jamie dropped inside her bedchamber.

On the heels of her nightmare, she had to fight the urge to embrace him. She stepped back, hugging herself to stop herself from doing just that.

"What are you doing here?" she whispered, glancing over her shoulder toward her door—expecting her father to barge inside.

"I talked to your father. Now I'm talking to you."

Her hands chafed her arms. "You shouldn't be here."

He advanced on her. "How else am I to learn if you're as foolish as your father?"

She backed away, lifting her chin a notch. "Don't malign my father."

"He's a good man. Just not very sensible. You're ruined if we don't wed, Paget. So is your father."

"Papa doesn't think I should rush to make a decision—"

He snorted and moved for her armoire.

She followed after him. "What are you doing?"

He pulled her valise out from the bottom. "Packing you."

"Packing? For what?"

"Gretna."

Her mouth sagged. It took her a moment to recover her voice. "You want to elope?"

His eyes gleamed down at her in the gloom. "Do you know a quicker way to wed in haste? Especially since your father's not very cooperative on the matter." He started rifling through her clothing. He glanced over his shoulder at her. "You should probably do this."

"No." The single word slipped from her mouth.

He stopped and turned, his head cocking to the side. "Be sensible, Paget."

"No. They only saw us kiss." She shook her head. "The gossip will fade."

He growled and closed the space between them, his hands closing over her arms. "Then I'll have to thoroughly and truly compromise you so there is no doubt in your mind."

His hands flexed on her arms, singeing her through the sleeves of her nightgown. She felt his gaze on her face . . . her lips. A secret thrill skated over her skin. She suppressed her shiver of excitement and gave a hard shake of her head.

She opened her mouth to deliver a ringing setdown, but the words never made it past her lips. His mouth crushed hers and her protest died in her throat.

There was no resistance. She tangled her hands in his hair, pulling his head closer, deepening their kiss and parrying her tongue with his. He backed her up until she bumped the bed.

He broke the kiss and her eyes fluttered open. Her chest rose and fell with each savage breath that shuddered free of her lungs. His eyes glittered at her in the dark. He gathered her nightgown into two fistfuls against her hips.

In a single, swift move, he pulled the nightgown over her head. The room's cool air rushed over her body and she shivered.

"Do you want me?" he said, breathing against her temple, stirring the fine hairs there.

She managed a strangled sound, a gurgled affirmation. *Want him?* With every fiber of her being.

His big hand cupped her bottom and lifted her high against him, nestling her against his prodding erection. He rounded the curve of her bottom, sliding lower, fingers teasing, probing her entrance and tearing a sharp gasp from her throat.

"What are you doing?"

"Seeing just how wet you are," he rasped against her neck.

Then she was falling. His body came down over hers, surrounding her, pinning her to the bed. Instinctively her legs parted wider, allowing him to settle deeper against her.

His hands cupped her face, held her as if she were the most precious thing in the world. Their mouths fused together, a hot, wet melding of lips and tongues, of nips and long, deep kisses.

His hands moved, slid over her. She let herself go, reveling in his mouth, his hands on her naked body. He pulled back, and she moaned in disappointment, watching his shadowy form as he shed his clothing. And then he was back. She sighed at the delicious sensation of his skin against hers.

He took her hand and moved it between them, guiding it to his manhood. An incredible sense of freedom, of power, seized her.

"Touch me," he drawled in a voice she hardly recognized, so deep and guttural. Harsh with need.

Her hand closed around his hard length. Her breath came faster. He was bigger than she had imagined. The skin softer.

His groan emboldened her. A shudder ran through him and vibrated within her as she pumped her hand over him—slowly, carefully at first, then in long, firm strokes that made him breathe harder. She rubbed her thumb over his tip, delighted at his low groan, at the bead of moisture that rose up to kiss her thumb and coat the head of him.

Releasing him, she shoved hard at his chest. He fell back on the bed. She hovered over him for a moment, wishing she could see the magnificence of his body. She traced the ridges of muscles along his stomach, the outline of each rib. The overwhelming, scandalous urge to taste him overcame her. Just as he had tasted her breasts, she wanted to taste every inch of his body.

Tentatively, she dipped her head and tongued his navel . . . before licking her way down a thin line of hair leading to that part of him that made her belly tighten and clench in anticipation.

She stopped, perched uncertainly over him. The rasp of his breath filled the air, encouraging her. As if he knew what she was contemplating, he pleaded, "Taste me."

Taking him in one hand, she placed a soft kiss at the tip of him.

"Paget," he choked in a voice she had never heard from him. Vulnerable. Lost. Totally at her mercy. It thrilled and aroused her, emboldening her as nothing else could. Slowly, she dipped her head and licked him.

His body jerked almost as if in pain.

She quickly released him. "Did I hurt you?"

In response, hard hands clamped down on her arms. Before she could draw a breath she was on her back and he was between her thighs, spreading her wide for him.

"I can't wait, Paget."

"Yes," she gasped, tilting her hips up for him in an instinctive move.

Then he was there. Big and hard, easing into her. She panted at the sensation of him stretching her, filling her. He was too much. Her head rolled side to side on the bed. This was too much.

"Oh," she squeaked as he lodged himself the final bit, burying himself deeply inside her.

"Are you . . ." he croaked.

She nodded, a deep burn building between her legs. "Please, Jamie . . . don't stop!"

His mouth slammed over hers as he plunged in and out of her body. It was wild and uninhibited and like nothing she had ever dreamed. He took what he needed, pounding into her ruthlessly and she didn't care, because she wanted it, too. Needed it. Needed him.

Her hips rose to meet him and she cried out as he drove harder into her, gripping her hips as if she were a lifeline, the only thing that kept him grounded to earth. Her heart swelled even as she reminded herself that this wasn't love. Only lust. A broken heart lay in wait if she let herself believe this was more than that.

CHAPTER EIGHT

The instant Jamie felt her body tremble and arch under him in the throes of her climax, he knew that he would stop at nothing to convince this woman to marry him.

His own climax followed fast and fierce. He reveled in the sensation of himself spilling inside her, knowing nothing would please him more than creating children with her. And that's when it became blindingly clear. He was in love with Paget Ellsworth. He loved her. He would love only her for all of his days.

She breathed heavily beneath him, the tips of her breasts pebble-hard and rubbing his chest in the most arousing way, even after he just spent himself inside her.

He propped himself on his elbows and stayed just so, buried in her, never wanting to leave.

"Paget," he began, determined to hear her agree to become his wife. The need burned within him. He simply knew that he had to marry this woman, to wake up beside her every morning for the rest of his life.

"You should go." She pushed at his shoulder.

"I'll leave. Once I hear you say you will marry me."

A long pause fell, the only sound their rasping breaths and the rush of his blood in his ears. She had to agree. "As wonderful as this was . . . it's not enough, Jamie."

With a curse, he stood. *He* still wasn't enough. That's what she meant.

He paced in front of her bed, dragging a hand through his hair, desperation rising hot and ragged inside him. He wasn't his father. He wasn't Brand or Owen.

She slid to the edge of the bed, clutching the counterpane to her nakedness.

"I wonder," he began, "if your father would agree. Things have moved farther than a kiss, wouldn't you say? Will he still think you need more time to decide or would he take one look at you and think you've already made your decision?"

"You wouldn't do that," she whispered, staring up at him with her dark eyes, enormous and horrified.

He held her gaze for a long moment before moving for the door, desperation driving him.

"No!" She launched off the bed and jumped between him and the door. "Very well! Fine! I'll marry you," she hissed, the fury in her eyes killing something inside him.

He couldn't do this. He didn't want it be like this. He didn't want her this way. Shaking his head, he turned from her and snatched up his clothes. "Forget it. Never mind."

She tugged at his arm, urging him to face her. "Never mind?" she echoed, her voice incredulous . . . and furious. Her body fairly hummed with energy and he suspected she wanted to strike him. "I accepted your proposal, Jamie. What do you want from me?"

He flung his clothes to the floor and hauled her against him. "I want you to love me like I love you!"

If possible her dark eyes widened further. She trembled in his arms, her mouth falling into a small o.

With a curse, he released her, feeling like the worst sort of fool. He'd done it. Uttered the words that would be sure to drive her from him. Just like anyone else he had ever tried to love, she couldn't possibly want him in return.

Then she was in front of him, her hands seizing his face, dragging his mouth down to hers. She kissed him fiercely, whispering feverishly against his lips, "I do love you. I love you, Jamie."

Something broke loose inside him. He wrapped his arms around her, lifting her off her feet.

"Oh, Jamie, I do love you . . ." A shudder racked him as her lips spoke the sweet words against his mouth.

"When I first saw you outside the manor . . . I think I knew then." He chuckled against her lips. "Or perhaps it was the slap. That might have woken me to the fact that I've always been a little bit in love with you. Even before India. When we were children."

"Why didn't you tell me how you felt?" She lifted her head to demand, the indignant light returning to her dark eyes. "We could have saved ourselves time."

"Why didn't *you* tell me?" he countered, his lips lifting in a smile.

She shook her head, her pale hair a floating nimbus around her. She looked like an angel. His angel. His salvation. "Because I'm a fool."

"Well, I'm a fool, too," he said. "I didn't think I had a right to love you."

She smiled deeply. "Then we really are perfect for each other, aren't we? Because I didn't think you could love me."

"How could I not love you?" He nuzzled her neck, reveling in the sweet softness of her skin just below her ear. "I adore you, Paget Ellsworth."

She trailed her fingers through his hair. "Owen is a good person," she replied rather breathlessly as he placed an open-mouthed kiss right beside her ear. "He won't begrudge us. He'll understand."

He knew the words stemmed from her worry that Owen very well might begrudge them. That he might not ever understand. A great sigh eased from him as love for her flowed through him, free and fearless. "He'll have to. Because I love you, and nothing on this earth will ever make me sorry for that."

She smiled deeply. "That makes two of us."

EPILOGUE

One year later . . .

Paget turned the page of her book and smiled as her husband's hand idly caressed the slight swell to her belly. A log popped in the great hearth, crumbling with a spray of sparks. The wind howled against the windows. Inside the warm library, curled upon the soft fur rug with the man she loved, she had never felt so safe and content. Every day was this—as though nothing could touch the perfection of her world.

Jamie sat with his back propped against the couch, long legs stretched out before him. She rested her head on his lap and tried to focus on the page before her and not on the distracting man that filled her head with all manner of thoughts . . . thoughts far more appealing than the book of poetry in her hands.

Her gaze slid up from the page she was reading to glance at Jamie. As though he felt her gaze, his gaze drifted from the newspaper he was reading to look down at her.

"Is your leg numb yet?" she inquired.

"No, I like you here."

She covered his hand where it curved around her belly,

around their child. She smiled up at him invitingly, turning her cheek against his thigh. "You know . . . I can think of something else for us to do on a cold winter afternoon."

His sea-blue eyes darkened and he bent his head, taking her lips in a hot kiss.

A knock at the door brought his head back up with a growl.

"Come in," he called.

Mr. Jarvis stepped inside the room, his stiff form bearing a tray. "I thought you might wish to read the day's post, my lord."

His joints creaked as he moved forward, proffering the tray. Jamie accepted the several envelopes. Jarvis slipped from the room, the door clicking softly behind him.

"Now," Paget purred. "Where were we?" Her hand circled around her husband's neck to pull him back down, but something in his expression stopped her. "What is it?"

She followed his gaze to the letter sitting on top of the small pile of correspondence.

"It's from Owen."

Her smile slipped. They had not heard from Owen since Jamie returned home. There had been no response when they sent him news of their marriage. They had begun to fear the worst. She watched as her husband quickly ripped it open, not bothering to rise for a letter opener.

She waited, heart racing as he scanned the words. When he finished, he dropped the parchment to his lap. "Well?" she prompted unable to read his expression.

"Owen's coming home."

Ready to find out what happened to Owen,
the mysterious Earl of McDowell?
Here's a sneak peek at his story,

HOW TO LOSE A BRIDE IN ONE NIGHT,

available August 2013 from Avon Books.

An Excerpt from

HOW TO LOSE A BRIDE IN ONE NIGHT

Consciousness pulled at her. Eyes still closed, Annalise floated, flying, arms suspended at her sides.

A heavy, pulling throb in her head and a sharp sting in her ribs pawed at her consciousness—urging her to dive back into the comfort of oblivion. But something else nagged at her, urging her to wake up. A memory. Something she should not forget. It sank its teeth through the fog of her thoughts, hunting her.

Everything came back in a rush then. She stopped herself just short of opening her eyes. She tensed and then quickly forced the tension back out . . . purging it from every limb as she concentrated on lying perfectly still. *On not opening her eyes.*

A soft breeze swam over her. The hem of her nightgown fluttered at her calves and she knew she was outside. Still close to the water. She could hear it lapping the sides of the barge.

Cool hands held her. He was taking her somewhere. She knew without opening her eyes that it was Bloodsworth. Her husband. *Her murderer.* He thought he had killed her back in their cabin. Smothered her with a pillow. So where was he taking her now?

It was safe to assume he would finish his gruesome task once he realized she was still alive. She hung limply in his arms, not daring to so much as lift her chest to breathe. Her life depended on his belief that he held a corpse.

He came to a halt. It felt windier, standing in one place—wherever that was—no longer swaying with his movements. He adjusted her in his arms with the barest grunt. The moments stretched. The silence deafening. It took everything in her to play dead, to feign that she wasn't aware of his body holding her so closely, of the hands gripping her—the same ones that held a pillow down over her face just moments ago.

Then she was lowered unceremoniously, dropped to the hard deck. Her head hit with a hard thump, her neck snapping back sharply, but she schooled her features into a blank mask and bit the inside of her cheek to keep from crying out. The wind buffeted her, playing with the hem of her night rail.

His voice rolled over her, his tones as crisp and familiar as ever. "Well, we can't forget this, can we?"

He seized her hand, grabbing her ring finger tightly. His fingers pulled on the wedding band he had slid on only hours before. His grip was hard and merciless, twisting her finger in an unnatural direction in his effort to reclaim his family heirloom. "Don't want to give it up, do you, wife?"

She prayed the ring would just slide free and rid her of this agony. At last it slid off her finger.

The soles of Bloodsworth's boots scraped over the deck. She sensed him standing above her. His voice rang out in satisfaction. "There we go. Saved you from that nasty bit of rubbish."

She envisioned him standing over her and addressing his precious family ring. She was "*that nasty bit of rubbish.*" How could she have ever thought he cared for her? She should have known her bridal settlement was the only thing that attracted his suit. And perhaps she had known that, but she thought he at least *liked* her. Enough to keep her around. Enough not to *kill* her.

His arms came around her again. He hefted her up with a grunt. "Little cow, I'm thinking you'll sink straight to the bottom. Farewell, *wife*." The last word was uttered with such scathing scorn she marveled that he had stomached marrying her at all. The entire ceremony must have revolted him.

And then she was falling through air.

Plunging deep into the abyss. Water rushed up all around her, enveloping her. She gasped at the sudden cold, swallowing a mouthful of briny water for the effort.

She swam to the surface, breaking free with a ragged gasp. She dragged a deep breath into her aching lungs and tossed her head left and right against the swiftly moving waters, trying to clear the tangle of hair from her eyes.

The view had been deceptive from her window. The river had looked calm. Peaceful. But now that she was a captive of its freezing depths, the current sucked at her, carrying her away from her wedding barge.

She squinted against the night, marking the dark looming

shape of the barge, a hulking beast hunched over the waters that crept slowly away from her.

She detected Bloodsworth's figure at the railing, his face a shadowy smudge on the night. She watched as he turned and disappeared back into the bowels of the barge, free of a wife. Free of her.

Swallowing back her terror, she kicked, grateful at least that she could swim. The shore didn't look too far. Struggling to ignore the incessant ache in her ribs where Bloodsworth had struck her, she started swimming, working her arms and legs, only to discover that the shore was much farther than it looked, and the current was determined to keep her from it.

Choking, she strained to keep her head above the slapping waves. Her strong leg worked three times as hard and yet it wasn't enough. Her exhaustion grew, dragging her down. The current slapped at her face, continuing to pull at her, tugging her along. She went under again and again, popping back up only to suck in a wet breath.

Jagged shapes emerged in the water, first only a few and then more, increasing in frequency. Rocks. She jerked to avoid them, but there were too many. Her right foot scraped something sharp. She cried out and choked on water.

Suddenly pain slammed into her lame leg, spinning her. Suddenly she was confused, no longer sure what direction was up. Lancing pain shot up her limb, settling deep into her bone, reverberating to every nerve in her body.

She tried to kick her way to the surface. Agony screamed through her right leg, telling her something was wrong. Dreadfully wrong. She couldn't force it to move.

Gray edged at her vision, closing in. She couldn't do it anymore. Couldn't fight. Bloodsworth had succeeded after all.

She wasn't going to make it out of this river alive.

Owen squinted against the afternoon's gray sky, swaying loosely in his saddle as his mount meandered along the road. Never mind that it was overcast. The day was too bright for him. The effects of last night's binge with a bottle of brandy still bore its effects. Thousands of tiny hammers beat inside his head.

He scratched at his bristly jaw, unable to recall the last time he had shaved. Perhaps a week ago. He didn't care enough to correct the matter. He hadn't even cared enough to shave before arriving home into the loving embrace of his family. Not that he had stayed longer than a day. It took him all of five minutes in the company of Jamie and Paget to realize he couldn't stomach another day with either one of them.

His brother and bride were nauseatingly happy, and he was not fit company for happy people. It had nothing to do with the fact that his brother had wed Owen's childhood sweetheart. The discovery of Jamie and Paget happily wed might have surprised him if he allowed himself to consider events . . . but it had not overly concerned him. Not as it would have four years ago when he was besotted with Paget. When he possessed a heart. When he was more than the shell of a man that he was now.

He felt only relief to know that Paget had moved on—that she wasn't waiting for him. There was no disappointing her. Because *what* he was, *who* had become . . . there was no coming back from that.

The Owen whom Jamie and Paget once knew was dead. Lost halfway around the world.

His mount quickened its pace, and he knew he was approaching the river. Reaching its banks, he dismounted and led the horse to water, holding the reins loosely in his hand as it drank.

He scanned his surroundings, his gaze missing nothing on land or water. He might be in the land of his birth, a mere day's ride from London, but a part of him would always be back in India scouting for rebels. Ready to kill. A talent he had perfected these past few years. It turned out he was extraordinarily good at killing.

His gaze stopped, arresting on something several yards downriver. Everything inside him tightened with familiar alertness, his time as a soldier rushing to the surface.

Ever wary, he moved closer. At first, he thought it nothing more than a mound of fabric, discarded and washed ashore. Even soiled, the material was startling white alongside the muddy bank. But then he detected the shape of a body beneath the sopping wet fabric.

A female body.

She lay face down, a limp arm stretched above her head. One leg stretched out, its pale foot and calf disappearing into the ink of water. He took a slow look around, well aware that a trap could wait anywhere. She could be the bait some nefarious brigands left to lure unsuspecting travelers to a foul end.

The still and silent woods met his sweeping stare, the gentle slap of water the only sound. He pushed the ghosts from his head, burying the cries of dead men deep as he turned his attention back to the woman. He cautiously approached. Crouching, he carefully touched her shoulder and rolled her onto her back.

She was young. Her face ashen. Eyes closed, her lashes fanned out against her cheeks in dark crescents that looked almost obscene against her waxy, colorless skin.

He pressed his fingertips to her throat. Icy cold to the touch, her pulse hiccupped there, the smallest, barely there flutter. Soft as a moth's wings. Not good.

He leaned closer, listening for her breath. The air escaped her bloodless lips in tiny, hard-fought rasps. He compressed his lips.

His gaze skimmed her, assessing. Scratches, cuts, and bruises marred her pale skin. The hem of her gown was streaked in faint pink tinges of blood. He tugged the gown up, checking for injuries, wincing at the sight of her right leg. From the odd shape, it was clearly broken. A deep gash on her foot probably needed stitching as well. Owen glanced to the river and back at her, marveling that she was alive. Given her injuries, he couldn't quite fathom how she had not drowned.

Staring at her for a long moment, he brushed some of the brown hair from her forehead. "How'd you get in that river, hmm?"

His mind quickly worked, plotting the best way to find her help. He spent the last five years attacking *sepoys*, assassinating them at the behest of his commanders. He was about taking lives, not saving.

They were a day's ride from his family home—not that he wanted to return there again. The next village was a half day ride south. He'd planned on spending the night there before continuing on to London.

Sighing, he glanced around them again, suddenly wishing someone else would happen upon them. Someone better equipped to care for a female who didn't look as though she would live out the day.

"Come, little one," he murmured, slipping his arms beneath her, one under her legs and the other at her back, taking care not to jostle her wounded leg more than necessary.

Contrary to his words, she was no fragile bit of crystal. She was generously curved in his arms, and yet his six-foot-plus frame ate up the distance toward his horse as if she weighed nothing at all. After grueling conditions in India, she was a slight burden. Not when he had lived so long with pain and discomfort.

Remounting with her in his arms was a tricky task, but he managed it, laying her carefully across his lap. With her legs dangled off to one side, he grasped the reins and prodded his mount to move. Her head lolled against his chest, her face settling against his well-worn jacket. Almost trustingly, it seemed. Absurd, of course. She was unconscious.

Disconcerted, he blinked down at her. It was impossible to recall the last time a woman had fallen asleep in his arms. There'd been women in his life, in his bed, but no one that he actually *slept* with. No one he had held in his arms once he satisfied his body's need for them.

Looking up again, he urged his mount into a faster clip, eager to reach the next town and rid himself of this newfound burden. So that he could be on his way. Just him and the demons of his past.

The female in his arms stiffened with a sharp gasp.

Startled, he looked down to find himself staring into a

pair of brown eyes. Framed in lush lashes, the eyes were no ordinary brown. They were velvety . . . chocolate rimmed in the darkest black. They shined, luminous, as if lit from within. She stared directly at him, the fear there unmistakable.

His hand reached down to cup her face, trying to offer some comfort. "Don't be frightened. I mean you no harm."

Nothing in her wild, searching gaze indicated she understood or even heard him. Those eyes looked right through him, as though she were somewhere else entirely, caught up in a living nightmare. Her breath fell faster in sharp little pains.

"Easy," he soothed, not really knowing what sort of words he should say. He wasn't accustomed to doling out comfort or reassurances. He pressed a hand awkwardly over her forehead and made a hushing sound. The kind his old nanny used to make whenever he'd hurt himself.

Perhaps it worked. Or perhaps she was just out of her head with pain.

Her eyelids drifted shut. After a long moment, he looked back up at the road and urged his mount faster, suddenly determined that she *would* live out the day.

If you love Sophie Jordan's lush historical romances,
get ready to fall in love with her bestselling young adult
romance series,

FIRELIGHT,

available now from HarperTeen.

An Excerpt from

FIRELIGHT

Gazing out at the quiet lake, I know the risk is worth it.

The water is still and smooth. Polished glass. Not a ripple of wind disturbs the dark surface. Low-rising mist drifts off liquid mountains floating against a purple-bruised sky. An eager breath shudders past my lips. Soon the sun will break.

Azure arrives, winded. She doesn't bother with the kickstand. Her bike clatters next to mine on the ground. "Didn't you hear me calling? You know I can't pedal as fast as you."

"I didn't want to miss this."

Finally, the sun peeks over the mountains in a thin line of red-gold that edges the dark lake.

Azure sighs beside me, and I know she's doing the same thing I am—imagining how the early morning light will taste on her skin.

"Jacinda," she says, "we shouldn't do this." But her voice lacks conviction.

I dig my hands into my pockets and rock on the balls

of my feet. "You want to be here as badly as I do. Look at that sun."

Before Azure can mutter another complaint, I'm shucking off my clothes. Stashing them behind a bush, I stand at the water's edge, trembling, but not from the cold bite of early morning. Excitement shivers through me.

Azure's clothes hit the ground. "Cassian's not going to like this," she says.

I scowl. As if I care what he thinks. He's not my boyfriend. Even if he did surprise attack me in Evasive Flight Maneuvers yesterday and try to hold my hand. "Don't ruin this. I don't want to think about him right now."

This little rebellion is partly about getting away from him. *Cassian.* Always hovering. Always there. Watching me with his dark eyes. Waiting. Tamra can have him. I spend a lot of my time wishing he wanted her—that the pride would choose her instead of me. Anyone but me. A sigh shudders from my lips. I just hate that they're not giving me a choice.

But it's a long way off before anything has to be settled. I won't think about it now.

"Let's go." I relax my thoughts and absorb everything humming around me. The branches with their gray-green leaves. The birds stirring against the dawn. Clammy mist hugs my calves. I flex my toes on the coarse rasp of ground, mentally counting the number of pebbles beneath the bottoms of my feet. And the familiar pull begins in my chest. My human exterior melts away, fades, replaced with my thicker draki skin.

My face tightens, cheeks sharpening, subtly shifting, stretching. My breath changes as my nose shifts, ridges pushing out from the bridge. My limbs loosen and lengthen. The drag of my bones feels good. I lift my face to the sky. The clouds become more than smudges of gray. I see them as though I'm already gliding through them. Feel cool condensation kiss my body.

It doesn't take long. It's perhaps one of my quickest manifests. With my thoughts unfettered and clear, with no one else around except Azure, it's easier. No Cassian with his brooding looks. No Mom with fear in her eyes. None of the others, watching, judging, sizing me up.

Always sizing me up.

My wings grow, slightly longer than the length of my back. The gossamer width of them pushes free. They unfurl with a soft whisper on the air—a sigh. As if they, too, seek relief. Freedom.

A familiar vibration swells up through my chest. Almost like a purr. Turning, I look at Azure, and see she is ready, beautiful beside me. Iridescent blue. In the growing light, I note the hues of pink and purple buried in the deep blue of her draki skin. Such a small thing I never noticed before.

Only now I see it, in the break of dawn, when we are meant to soar. When the pride forbids it. At night you miss so much.

Looking down, I admire the red-gold luster of my sleek arms. Thoughts drift. I recall a chunk of amber in my family's cache of precious stones and gems. My skin looks like that now. Baltic amber trapped in sunlight. It's deceptive. My skin appears delicate, but it's as tough as armor. It's been a long time since I've seen myself this way. Too long since I've tasted sun on my skin.

Azure purrs softly beside me. We lock eyes—eyes with enlarged irises and dark vertical slits for pupils—and I know she's over her complaints. She stares at me with irises of glowing blue, as happy as I am to be here. Even if we broke every rule in the pride to sneak off protected grounds. We're here. We're free.

On the balls of my feet, I spring into the air. My wings snap, wiry membranes stretching as they lift me up.

With a twirl, I soar.

Azure is there, laughing beside me, the sound low and guttural.

Wind rushes over us and sweet sunlight kisses our flesh. Once we're high enough, she drops, descends through the air in a blurring tailspin, careening toward the lake.

My lip curls. "Show-off!" I call, the rumble of draki speech vibrating deep in my throat as she dives into the lake and remains underwater for several minutes.

As a water draki, whenever she enters water, gills appear on the side of her body, enabling her to survive submerged . . . well, forever, if she chooses. One of the many useful talents our dragon ancestors assumed in order to survive. Not all of us can do this, of course. *I* can't.

I do other things.

Hovering over the lake, I wait for Azure to emerge. Finally, she breaks the surface in a glistening spray of water, her blue body radiant in the air, wings showering droplets.

"Nice," I say.

"Let's see you!"

I shake my head and set out again, diving through the tangle of mountains, ignoring Azure's "c'mon, it's so cool!"

My talent is *not* cool. I would give anything to change it. To be a water draki. Or a phaser. Or a visiocrypter. Or an onyx. Or . . . Really, the list goes on.

Instead, I am this.

I breathe fire. The only fire-breather in the pride in more than four hundred years. It's made me more popular than I want to be. Ever since I manifested at age eleven, I've ceased to be Jacinda. Instead, I'm fire-*breather*. A fact that has the pride deciding my life as if it's theirs to control. They're worse than my mother.

Suddenly I hear something beyond the whistling wind and humming mists of the snow-capped mountains at every side. A faint, distant sound.

My ears perk. I stop, hovering in the dense air.

Azure cocks her head; her dragon eyes blink, staring hard. "What is it? A plane?"

The noise grows, coming fast, a steady beat now. "We should get low."

Nodding, Azure dives. I follow, glancing behind us, seeing only the jagged cropping of mountains. But hearing more. Feeling more.

It keeps coming.

The sound chases us.

"Should we go back to the bikes?" Azure looks back at me, her blue-streaked black hair rippling like a flag in the wind.

I hesitate. I don't want this to end. Who knows when we can sneak out again? The pride watches me so closely, Cassian is always—

"Jacinda!" Azure points one iridescent blue finger through the air.

I turn and look. My heart seizes.

A chopper rounds a low mountain, so small in the distance, but growing larger as it approaches, cutting through the mist.

"Go!" I shout. "Drop!"

I dive, clawing wind, my wings folded flat against my body, legs poised arrow straight, perfectly angled for speed.

But not fast enough.

The chopper blades beat the air in a pounding frenzy. *Hunters.* Wind tears at my eyes as I fly faster than I've ever flown before.

Azure falls behind. I scream for her, glancing back, reading the dark desperation in her liquid gaze. "Az, keep up!"

Water draki aren't built for speed. We both know that. Her voice twists into a sob and I hear just how well she knows it in the broken sound. "I'm trying! Don't leave me! Jacinda! Don't leave me!"

Behind us, the chopper still comes. Bitter fear coats my mouth as two more join it, killing any hope that it was a random helicopter out for aerial photos. It's a squadron, and they are definitely hunting us.

Is this how it happened with Dad? Were his last moments like this? Tossing my head, I shove the thought away. I'm *not* going to die today—my body broken and sold off into bits and pieces.

I nod to the nearing treetops. "There!"

Draki never fly low to the ground, but we don't have a choice.

Azure follows me, weaving in my wake. She pulls close to my side, narrowly missing the flashing trees in her wild fear. I stop and drift in place, chest heaving with savage breath. The choppers whir overhead, their pounding beat deafening, stirring the trees into a frothing green foam.

"We should demanifest," Az says, panting.

As if we could. We're too frightened. Draki can never hold human form in a state of fear. It's a survival mechanism. At our core we're draki; that's where we derive our strength.

I peer up through the latticework of shaking branches shielding us, the scent of pine and forest ripe in my nostrils.

"I can get myself under control," Az insists in our guttural tongue.

I shake my head. "Even if that's true, it's too risky. We have to wait them out. If they see two girls out here . . . after they just spotted two female draki, they might get suspicious." A cold fist squeezes around my heart. I can't let that happen. Not just for me, but for everyone. For draki everywhere. The secret of our ability to appear as humans is our greatest defense.

"If we're not home in the next hour, we're busted!"

I bite my lip to stop from telling her we have more to worry about than the pride discovering we snuck out. I don't want to scare her even more than she already is.

"We have to hide for a little—"

Another sound penetrates the beating blades of a chopper. A low drone on the air. The tiny hairs at my nape tingle. Something else is out there. Below. On the ground. Growing closer.

I look skyward, my long talonlike fingers flexing open and shut, wings vibrating in barely controlled movement. Instinct urges flight, but I know they're up there. Waiting. Circling buzzards. I spy their dark shapes through the treetops. My chest tightens. They aren't going away.

I motion Az to follow me into the thick branches of a towering pine. Folding our wings close to our bodies, we shove amid the itchy needles, fighting the scraping twigs. Holding our breath, we wait.

Then the land comes alive, swarming with an entourage of vehicles: trucks, SUVs, dirt bikes.

"No," I rasp, eyeing the vehicles, the men, armed to the teeth. In a truck bed, two men crouch at the ready, a great net launcher before them. Seasoned hunters. They know what they're doing. They know what they're hunting.

Az trembles so badly the thick branch we're crouched on starts to shake, leaves rustling. I clutch her hand. The dirt bikes lead the way, moving at a dizzying speed. A driver of one SUV motions out the window. "Look to the trees," he shouts, his voice deep, terrifying.

Az fidgets. I clutch her hand harder. A bike is directly below us now. The driver wears a black T-shirt that hugs his young muscled body. My skin tightens almost painfully.

"I can't stay here," Az chokes out beside me. "I've got to go!"

"Az," I growl, my low rumbling tones fervent, desperate. "That's what they want. They're trying to flush us out. Don't panic."

Her words spit past gritted teeth. "I. Can't."

And I know with a sick tightening of my gut that she's not going to last.

Scanning the activity below and the choppers cutting across the sky above, I make up my mind right then.

"All right." I swallow. "Here's the plan. We separate—"

"No—"

"I'll break cover first. Then, once they've gone after me, you head for water. Go under and stay there. However long it takes."

Her dark eyes gleam wetly, the vertical lines of her pupils throbbing.

"Got it?" I demand.

She nods jerkily, the ridges on her nose contracting with a deep breath. "W-what are you going to do?"

I force a smile, the curve of my lips painful on my face. "Fly, of course."